RAM

EROTICA FOR HIM

RAM is published bi-monthly by Sweet Nothings.

RAM: Erotica for Him
Issue #1 July/August 2014
Copyright © 2014 Sweet Nothings
Published by Sweet Nothings

CONTENTS

STORIES

A Little Fun..1
Helping Hand...12
Room Service...24
The Lucky One..47
Impure Thoughts...69

RAMBLINGS (LETTERS)

Service with a Smile....................................82
Sharing is Caring..86
Changing it Up..91

TIPS & TRICKS..95

END QUOTE...98

From the Editor

Welcome to the premiere issue of RAM Digest, a new, bi-monthly collection of erotica and non-fiction just for men.

What makes RAM just for men? Once you start reading it'll be easy to see why, but in a nutshell it's erotica with a focus on sex and situations that appeal to the male psyche. It features fiction stories, real letters from people just like you, as well as tips & tricks offered by our perverted staff to help improve your skills in the bedroom.

And hey, if some women get a kick out of it and like what we have to offer, then that's great! We're not going to complain about anyone reading RAM, so long as they enjoy themselves.

Our hope is that RAM will reach thousands of men who enjoy getting off either by themselves, or with a partner. The content inside these pages is meant to turn you on, and to open your mind to new possibilities when it comes to sex. You might read something you haven't thought of before and want to try it out, or you might find something useful in our tips & tricks section that makes you a better lover. Whatever the case may be, we want men to take something away from each issue and put it into practice, be it with a lover, or inside their heads when they're accessing hot and sweaty fantasies to masturbate to. It's all good.

So I hope you enjoy the first issue of RAM and

come back in a couple of months for more. Over time we'd like to feature more content from readers, both in our RAMBLINGS letters section, and in our TIPS & TRICKS section, or maybe we'll create a whole new FEEDBACK section that's just you letting us know what you want more of, or what we can improve upon. Feel free to email us your ideas and letters at *ramdigest@gmail.com*. Eventually we'll have a website set-up, but for now that's the best way to get in touch with us.

Now sit back, grab some tissues, and prepare to be turned on with RAM: Erotica for Him.

Enjoy!

Kelly Haven
May 30, 2014

A LITTLE FUN

When my wife took off and left me with our newborn son I thought for sure that my life was over. How was I going to raise a child all on my own, work, and meet someone that could possibly one day be his stepmother? I just couldn't see that happening. I was too busy changing diapers, potty training, and running myself ragged to ever see the forest through the trees.

Eventually, though, things turned around, and I got back on the horse when Ben was old enough to spend time with a babysitter. I started dating again. Going out and meeting new women that might one day be the future Mrs. Fowler. I had some good times, even got laid once in a while, but none of the girls I dated were mother material.

It's hard being a single father and trying to date because you can't just take into consideration your needs. You have to take into consideration the needs of your child as well. Your date might be a nice girl to you, but how is she with kids? Does she even like kids, or is she just pretending and really waiting for the first chance she gets to smack your baby around like they do on one of those hidden camera nanny shows? It's enough to drive a guy insane.

Needless to say that whole way of thinking put me on the biggest dry spell of my life. It had been nearly a year since I'd seen any action, and my latest date was no exception. She was nice enough; had a great body and tits to die for, but she had no personality. We just didn't hit it off.

I came home earlier than expected to my babysitter, Rachel, sitting on the couch watching some TV show. Ben was already in bed, and she was there with a big bowl of popcorn, just chilling out in her sweats and a t-shirt.

I've known Rachel since she was sixteen and moved into the neighborhood with her folks. They live four houses down from me and she was my go to babysitter when I had a date, or just needed a break from fatherhood for a couple of hours. She's a sweet girl, but she's no longer sixteen, that's for sure.

It was a little disheartening when she went off to college. I trusted Rachel with Ben, so finding someone to replace her was a bit of a pain. I must have gone through five sitters—three of which decided that my house was party central, and two that thought it would be okay to grope around with their boyfriends—before I found someone semi-reliable.

That's why I was ecstatic to learn that Rachel was home for the summer after completing her first year studies. It gave me a chance to relax a bit on my dates, and be myself without having to worry about what was going on back at home.

"Hi, Mr. Fowler," she said when I came in. "You're home early." She put the bowl of popcorn on the coffee table and wiped her fingers on her sweat pants.

"Hi Rachel. Yeah, we didn't really hit it off."

She gave me her sad eyes and batted her lashes, pouting at me. "I'm sorry."

That made me laugh, something I desperately needed in that moment. "Plenty of fish in the sea, right?" I asked.

She sucked in her cheeks and moved her lips like a fish, making us both laugh then.

I took a seat beside her on the couch and sighed. Rachel looked at me and I held her gaze for a moment, admiring her bright green eyes, smooth skin, and thin lips. She really is a tremendously beautiful young girl. I found myself thinking that I bet she doesn't have any trouble getting laid. College boys must be all over her.

I cleared my throat and glanced at the television. "What are you watching?" I asked.

"HBO," she said. "We don't have this channel in the dorms, so I thought I'd catch up on some shows I've missed while away, but since you're home now I guess I'll take off."

I waved my hand at and her and said, "Stay, it's fine. I could use the company."

"You sure?"

"Yeah. Watch your show."

"Cool. You want some popcorn?"

She grabbed the bowl off the table and held it out to me. "Sure," I said, taking a couple of pieces and popping them into my mouth, never taking my eyes off of hers.

We sat there together for a while, the scent of popcorn and Rachel's vanilla perfume filling the air around me. It had been a while since I'd felt this comfortable around a member of the opposite sex, and even though she was thirteen years my junior, it still felt nice.

Eventually, whatever she was watching started getting hot and heavy. I mean, really hot and heavy. Like softcore porn hot and heavy. I should have known when she said she was watching HBO. Most of their shows are filled with sex, and since it had been a while since I'd had any, it didn't take me long to get turned on watching the people on TV while indulging in my own fantasies.

Fantasies that, since she was sitting right next to me, involved Rachel.

I quickly glanced at her to see her reaction to watching something like that with me beside her, and her eyes were fixated on the television while she chewed her bottom lip ever so softly.

I thought about those soft lips wrapped around the bulge in my pants, which was growing and growing until it ached for some sweet release.

Taking a chance on things, I sat back on the couch and spread my legs a little, making it obvious how I felt. When the sex scene on TV was over, I saw Rachel out of the corner of my eye steal a look in my direction. She smiled, which was a good thing, and tucked a few strands of her dirty blonde hair behind her ear before inching her way closer to me until our shoulders were touching and she was leaning into me while still looking at the television.

I closed my eyes and felt her hot breath on my neck. My cock twitched with lustful anticipation and she must have noticed it moving beneath the fabric of my jeans, because moments later I felt her cup her small hand between my legs and give me a nice, hard, squeeze. I gasped and opened my eyes to see her staring at me, smiling. A look of seductive playfulness in her eyes.

"Do you want me to suck your cock?" she asked.

I nodded, unable to find any words in that moment.

She started unbuckling me and her fingers had no trouble getting me undone. Rachel whipped my belt out of its loops and threw it to the floor. She giggled, and got down on her knees in front of me.

"Let's take these off," she said, tugging on my pants.

I didn't have to be asked twice. I unbuttoned them and she unzipped me, and before I knew it my jeans were around my ankles and my cock was swaying back and forth in front of her face.

"Mr. Fowler," she marveled. "It's so big."

I chuckled, words still escaping me, and watched as Rachel licked the palm of her hand before wrapping it around my girth, stroking up and down. Slowly at first, then faster and faster. She worked it over my swollen head, around my balls...everywhere. She hadn't even put her mouth on it yet and already I felt like I was going to explode in her face, that's how good it felt.

"You want me to suck it?" she asked in a breathy, tantalizing voice, her lips just inches from my cock.

I nodded, but that wasn't good enough for her.

"Tell me," she commanded. "Tell me what you want me to do."

I swallowed, hard, and moaned, "I want you to suck my cock. Please."

God, she had me in the palm of her hand—literally.

Without further torture, Rachel eagerly stroked me into her mouth, wrapping her lips tight around my shaft. She moved up and down with slow precision, trying to take as much of me down her throat as she could, which was damn near all of my dick. She gagged and came up for air, a tendril of saliva stretching from the tip of me to her bottom lip. She took it in her palm and stroked it up and down my shaft, getting me nice and slick.

"You like it messy?" she asked, winking at me.

Before I could say anything though, she dipped down low and scooped one of my testicles in her mouth, sucking it gently. She moved to the other one, rolling it across her tongue before tugging on the skin with her closed lips, all the while continuing to stroke my cock with her slick hand. It felt amazing, and I groaned with delight the more she serviced me.

"You keep that up and I'm going to end up

cumming in your mouth," I told her.

Rachel put my cock against the side of her cheek, as if peeking out from behind it, and raised her eyebrows. "That's the idea," she purred.

She sucked me back then, really going to work on my rock hard tool. She licked and sucked like a woman possessed, and I loved watching as her young mouth moved all over me. Up and down, back and forth; she coated me in her saliva until my shaft and balls were drenched in her goo and her chin gleamed with spit. It was incredible. I'd never had a blowjob like it before, and while I wanted it to last well into the night, I just couldn't hold out much longer. I felt my balls tighten and my cock pulsed with the anticipation of releasing a load into Rachel's mouth.

Where she had learned to suck dick like that is beyond me, but I wasn't complaining.

As if sensing my eminent release, she cupped my scrotum in her one palm and stroked me with the other, all the while keeping her lips wrapped around my bulbous head. Her cheeks contracted and expanded as she sucked, and my breathing became more labored as I was brought to the edge. With a final grunt I grabbed the back of her head and held on tight as I squirted hot jets of jizz down her throat. She mewed and accepted it all, bringing her eyes up to meet mine as she swallowed my cum, making my dick spasm with sheer pleasure.

"Mmm," Rachel moaned after swallowing every last drop. "That was a lot of cum, Mr. Fowler."

I smiled and wiped beaded sweat off my forehead, while Rachel continued to stroke my softening cock.

"It's been a while," I said.

"Tell me about it," she answered. "I don't even remember the last time I had a dick in my mouth."

"Seriously? I would have thought you'd have all kinds of boys after you in college."

"No time," she said, sitting back up on the couch beside me. "Between my classes and studying, there isn't room for anything else in my life."

Not one to be selfish, I kicked off my jeans and knelt down on the floor in front of Rachel. She seemed surprised at first, but when I began tugging off her sweat pants, she quickly softened to my touch and let me remove them for her. She had on a pair of boy short panties that clung tight to her body, outlining the mound between her legs, and I ran my hand over it, feeling the heat emanating off of her.

Without saying anything else, she peeled off her t-shirt to reveal a pair of the most spectacular breasts I have ever seen. There was no bra to cup them, and they hung freely before me. Perky and smooth, with rosy nipples that stood at attention. I reached out and took the soft globes in my hand, massaging them with care before sliding my tongue over them. I took one nipple in my mouth, and then moved to the other, sucking them gently. Tugging back on them with my lips, listening to Rachel gasp with delight.

Before long, I moved between her legs and licked her inner thighs, causing her to squeal and giggle.

"That tickles," Rachel laughed.

I smiled up at her and removed her panties,

tossing them to the floor beside me. Her pussy was petite and shaved, and already moist to the touch. I pressed my tongue against her clit and rolled it around a little, tasting the sweetness of her nectar on my buds.

"You like that?" I teased in the same manner she had done to me.

Rachel nodded, her eyes staring hungrily back into mine.

I spread her pussy lips with my thumbs and looked at the glistening, pink flesh on display. It was so young and tender, and I eagerly dove into it, licking up and down her slit. Rachel ran her thin fingers through my hair and pressed me harder between her spread-eagle legs. My tongue glided across every inch of her before I poked the tip of it in her tight hole. She whimpered at that, so I slid as much of it inside her as I could, wiggling it around between her slick walls. Grinding against me, I became coated in her juices—my chin and upper lip wet with sauce.

"Oh fuck that feels good," she moaned. "So fucking good."

The sound of Rachel's filthy mouth turned me on even more than licking her sweet snatch. I reached down between my legs and started stroking my cock to fruition again, all the while lapping up her dripping wet cunt over and over. She tasted amazing, and the thought of being inside her tight pussy was enough to get me hard again in seconds.

"I want to fuck you," I told her while sucking back on her clit.

"Do it from behind," she moaned.

I stood up with a rock hard erection and watched her get on all fours on the couch. I quickly got in behind her and slapped my cock against her ass cheeks.

"Naughty boy," Rachel giggled.

I slid into her, slowly, feeling her swallow every inch of my girth. She was so tight, and her pussy wrapped around me like a vice and I squeezed my eyes shut when I was all the way in, and held myself there for a moment before sliding back and forth, watching my cock go in and out of her.

"Do it harder," she begged.

Not one to disappoint, I grabbed hold of her ass and thrust myself as deep as I could go again and again. Our flesh clapped together and my balls swung against her clit over and over. A white sheen of cream covered my shaft the more we fucked, and I tugged back on her hair, bucking up against her. Rachel cried out as she came, and I grunted as she became even wetter. I let go of her hair and reached around to cup her tits in my hands, pinching her nipples between thumb and forefinger, while nibbling on her earlobe. My cock slid out of her, surprising the both of us. We laughed and she moaned for me to put it back. I did, really hammering away at her cunt then. Slamming into her repeatedly until her ass was red and I wanted nothing more than to explode all over her cheeks.

"Cum inside me," she said, causing me to slow down.

"You sure?"

"It's okay, I'm on the pill."

I sped up, burying myself deep inside her

pussy. The smell of sex filled the air around me and I trembled as my senses tingled at the aroma. My cock was aching to be set free so I pounded and pounded Rachel's amazing body until I just couldn't take it anymore and I flooded her insides with my hot cum. My dick twitched and spasmed inside her as I emptied myself deep in her tight hole, and listened to her moans of ecstasy while she buried her face in the couch cushions.

When every last drop was squeezed from my cock, I pulled out and collapsed down on the couch. Rachel sat up and snuggled next to me and we sat there for a while, catching our breaths and letting the cool air dry our sweaty bodies.

"Wow," she finally said after a few minutes.

"Yeah," I smiled, and kissed the top of her head.

"I can't wait to babysit for you again."

I laughed and sat up, reaching for my jeans. Just the thought of doing that again with her filled me with excitement, and I couldn't wait until my next date, when she had to come over and sit for me.

Don't get me wrong, I have no ideas about ever marrying Rachel. We're just having some fun, and sometimes...a little fun is all you need.

HELPING HAND

Hey there baby, how are you? Good, I hope. Listen, I know we just met but I was really, really hoping that you could help me out with something. You see, I'm only eighteen and I've had so little experience with boys that I think it's time I get a real man to show me the ropes. Would you be my real man?

You will? Awesome!

That makes me so happy because my ex-boyfriend said that I should learn more about sex before I even think of having it again, but what I really want to do is learn more about cock, and how to play with it. I think I could be really good at it given the chance, but I need to know what real men like, so do you think I could watch you play with yourself for a while? I promise I won't bite, unless you want me to.

Don't be shy. You'd really be helping me out. I saw you the other day and I couldn't help but notice the bulge in your pants. You must be so big, and I think I need a big cock to show me what to do. So come on, pull it out and let me see it.

What's the matter, are you nervous? Don't be. Here, I'll take off my clothes so you don't feel so bad.

My name's Emily, by the way.

What's yours?

Do you like my tight body? It's only eighteen years old. Here, let me turn around so you can see my ass.

Do you like it? Would you like to touch it? Go ahead.

Mmm...that feels nice. Let me take off my shorts so you can get a better look. Just let me undo this button, and zip down the fly. God, they're so tight. I don't know even know how I got them on. Wait, I'll bend over, that will help. Do you like it when I bend over? I know you do.

There. Off they go.

I know I should be nervous at you seeing me in my underwear like this, but I actually kind of like it. See my panties? I bought them fresh just for you. They're white with little fruits on them. Nice, huh? So soft and warm, and they hug my pussy just perfect. Can you see my little ass better now? I knew you'd like it. Not many girls have an ass like this. It's so smooth and creamy and young. Don't forget young. Do you like young girls? I hope so, because I like older men like you.

Here, let me turn around again and take off my top. Are you feeling better about this yet? I definitely am. It's exciting, knowing that I get to watch you stroke your big, hard dick. It turns me on so much. I can feel my pussy getting wetter by the second.

Okay, here it goes. I'll take off my top if you take off your pants. Deal?

Good. I knew you'd go for that. You just can't resist my tight body, can you? I don't blame you. Sometimes I just stand and stare at myself naked in the mirror before touching myself. It's so hot. So young.

You got your pants off yet? No? What are you waiting for? Are you waiting for me? Okay, okay. I'll go first. I bought this tank top just for you, too. See the way it clings to my body and shows off my tits? They're so firm and perky, and my pink nipples are already hard, but don't worry, I have a bra on. Just let me take this top off...

There. See? My bra matches my panties. I know that my tits aren't the biggest, but they're still a handful. Maybe I'll let you play with them later if you're good. Would you like that? Would you like to feel my young tits in your strong hands? I sure would. I love strong hands.

What do you think of my body? Be honest. Some of the other girls say I'm a little skinny for my height, but I don't think so. I think it looks sexy. My flat stomach, smooth skin, cute little ass...it all fits, right? Maybe later I'll let you see me naked. I bet you'd like that. My pussy is completely shaved and smells so good. God, I'm so wet just thinking about it.

First, though, I need to see you. So get those pants off and we'll get started.

There you go. Not so nervous now, are you? Good boy. I like your underwear, and is that a chub? Are you already getting hard? My, you are horny. That's good. I like being horny with you. I think it'll go better if we're both turned on. I'm tingling all over; see the goosebumps all over my body? On my tight little ass? So hot.

Okay, now it's time to pull out your dick. I really want to see the way you play with yourself so I can learn how to touch a man better. You're already halfway there, so you may as well just go all the way. Take off your underwear for me.

That's it. There you go. Feels nice, doesn't it? They way the cool air hits your...

Oh. My. God.

Look at your cock, it's so big. Holy shit. I suspected as much but seeing it like that is a little overwhelming. Are all men that big? How on earth could something so huge fit in my tight hole? Or even in my mouth? God, I have a lot to learn.

I'm sorry, I didn't mean to get flustered like that. I just...wow. I just saw you and freaked out. Forgive me?

Thank you.

Now, let me see you touch it. I'll just sit next to you and watch, okay? Do you like the way I smell? I use strawberry body lotion; it makes my skin so soft and shiny.

Close your eyes and take a deep breath.

Smells good, doesn't it?

Does it turn you on? It looks like it. Your cock is getting bigger and you haven't even started stroking it yet. Why don't you do that for me, right now?

Please?

Excellent.

See, that's not so bad. Having a hot, young, eighteen year old girl does wonders for a guy, right? Especially when she's sitting next to you in her underwear. That's it, baby. Stroke that cock for me. I like the way your hand travels up and down the shaft like that. It's so fluid. I'll have to remember to do that. What about the head? Do you play with that, too? Yeah? Oh, I see the way you run your hand all around it, squeezing gently. It seems to get you even harder. How nice! It's so purple, and throbbing. God, what I wouldn't give to taste it, but we're not here for that right now. I want to see you jack off. I want to watch as you stroke that big, hard cock for me.

That's it. Spit on your hand and rub it all around.

It's so slick when you do that. Makes your hand slide easier along your fucking cock. God, look at it. That's so damn hot. And your balls. They're so awesome. Do you play with those, too? Show me. Show me how you play with your balls, rolling them around in one hand while stroking the shaft with the other. Yeah, that's it baby. I see what you like now. Even your balls are wet with your saliva. Don't you wish it was my saliva? Don't you wish that your cock was in my young mouth right now? Well too bad. You can't have that yet. Maybe another time. I'm having too much fun watching you stroke yourself. It turns me on so much.

Do you mind if I spread my legs and touch myself while you do that? I can do it right beside you if you'd like. Yeah? Okay, just let me stand up and take off my panties for you. You've been waiting for this, haven't you? I sure have. I'll just slide them off...ta-da! Hehehe, you make me giggle like a schoolgirl. See how smooth my ass is? I told you. Here, I'll let you touch it just this once. Put your hand right here.

There. Feels good, right? So firm and soft. Squeeze it a little. Like a ripe orange. Mmm...I love your hands running all over my tight ass. Don't you?

Want to see my pussy?

I'll just sit back down next to you and spread my legs and you keep stroking your cock for me. Okay?

Good boy.

That's it, stroke it harder. Faster.

Here, take a look at my beautiful pussy. See, I told you it was shaved. Completely bald. Look at how wet it is. I'll spread my lips a little so you can see my pink. You like that? You like my young, pink pussy? It's so tight and wet. Look at the way it glistens in the light. Especially when I smear my juices all around it. That feels so good. When I brush my clit, it sends little shockwaves up through my whole body and makes me tremble. Like this.

Oh fuck, that feels so good.

Don't stop stroking yourself, baby. Your cock is so fucking hard. Like a rock. Now I know what men like. Up and down the shaft, just like that. Spit on your hand some more for me. Fuck yeah, that's so hot. Look at the way you play with your throbbing head. That's perfect. A good tip to learn for me. Holy fuck, I just love touching myself while watching you do that. Here, let me rest one of my legs on your knee so I can spread them further.

Keep stroking yourself.

My pussy is so wet, baby. I think I'll slip a finger inside it just for you. Do you like watching me as much as I like watching you? I sure hope so. It looks like it, judging from the size of your dick. That thing is huge. Watch as my finger slides inside me, okay?

Ohhhh fuck, that feels so amazing. I'm imagining that it's your cock sliding deep in my tight pussy. Does that make you feel good? Going in and out, just like my finger's doing right now. So tight. So wet.

Stroke your cock in motion with my finger. Pretend that's my pussy wrapped around you instead of your hand. Nice and warm, hugging your shaft. Up and down it slides, lips firm and tight around your big cock, and since I'm shaved you can watch every inch go deeper and deeper.

Do you like that? Do you like imagining my pussy while you jack off? I like thinking of you while I play with myself. It feels so right. So good. Does my leg feel good on yours? Is it soft? It better be. Nice and smooth, like the rest of me. I like spreading my legs for you so you can see my young, eighteen year old pussy. It gets me all hot and bothered knowing that you're staring at it while stroking your cock. Pretty soon you're going to explode all over, aren't you?

I can't wait.

Just keep stroking yourself stud, and I'll keep playing with my pussy. I'm learning a lot watching you do that. The way your hand slides up and down the shaft, the way you play with your balls and head; it's quite the learning experience for me. Maybe one day I'll get to do that for you. Would you like that? Would you like me to stroke your cock for you one day? Feel my tiny hands wrapped about your girth, moving it up and down, spitting on you all nasty-like? Mmm...I'd love that.

One day.

First I want to see you finish. I love the way your hand moves in long, fast strokes. Up and down, from base to tip. Keep licking your hand so that it stays nice and wet, imagining that it's my pussy. God, you're so hard, and my finger is so deep inside my pink pussy. I like wiggling it around in there, pretending that it's a tongue. Maybe one day it'll be your tongue. Would you like that? Would you like to taste me?

Oh God, I touched my clit. I think I'm going to have to keep that up. I want us to cum together, don't you? I'm starting to get that warm feeling in the pit of my stomach. All tight and hot, like a fresh ball of excitement waiting to gush out of me. I love to cum. I want to cum with you. You like cumming with young girls watching? I think that's so fucking hot.

Keep stroking yourself and we'll cum together, okay?

God, look at us. We're both breathing heavier. Our chests are both heaving up and down. Fuck, I love playing with my clit right next to you. Rubbing it around and around, faster and faster. Just like you're doing with the head of your cock. Mmm...it feels so fucking amazing, baby. I'm so wet that you can hear my juices slosh around my pussy. I love that sound. I love the clicking sound your hand is making on your cock, too. What with all the spit on it and everything. I wish it was my spit. I wish I was sucking on you right now so that you could cum in my mouth. Not yet, though. One day. For now I just want us to cum together, okay? Can you do that for me?

That's it baby. Keep stroking. I'm almost there. You with me?

Oh fuck. Oh fuck. Ohfuckohfuckohfuck...yeah baby. That's it. I love watching you stroke that fucking cock. Do it. Do it faster. Jerk that fucking cock for me while I play with my pussy. Holy shit that's hot. Stroke it. Up and down while I play with myself harder and faster. God, I'm about ready to cum. I can feel it in me, waiting to be unleashed out of my pussy. There's so much of it building up. Do you have a lot of cum, too? Deep in your balls? Waiting to break free? I want to see it shoot out of your dick and all over.

Keep stroking.

I love cum so much. I love it all over my body. In my mouth. Swallowing it. That's the best. I'll swallow your cum one day if you'd like. Yeah, would you like that? Would you like me to swallow your cum?

Fuck yeah; my pussy is so fucking hot right now. It's steaming. I can't wait to fucking cum with you. Oh God, around and around go my fingers. Everything down there is sopping wet between my legs. I can feel my juices dripping down the crack of my ass. It feels so good.

Come on, baby. Let's do this. Let's cum together.

Stroke it harder. Faster. Up and down, up and down. That's it baby. Jerk that cock for me. I love to watch it. I can see your balls tightening up with so much cum in them. You ready to shoot that hot load all over? Yeah, let's go. Let's do it. Let's fucking cum.

Oh fuck. Here I go baby. Just a few more seconds. My fingers feel so fucking amazing all over my clit. I'm thinking of you. Of your cock rubbing all over me. Of your tongue flicking back and forth over my eighteen year old pussy. Oh fuck, yeah. Yes! Yes! Yes!

Ohhhhh fuuuuuuuuuck.

Oh God. Oh God. Oh God. I'm cumming so fucking hard. Oh yes. It's gushing out of my pussy right now. All over. Fuck, it feels so good.

Oh and look at you. You're right there, too. Come on, baby. Cum for me. Stroke it out. All over. There you go. Up and down. Imagine my mouth over you, sucking harder and harder. Cum in my mouth sweetheart. Shoot all that hot, delicious cum down my throat. There it is, there it is!

Oh fuck, look at it all shoot all over the place. That's so damn sexy. There's so much of it, too. Such a big load. You even got some on my leg. Yeah, keep stroking that cock while you cum. Do it.

Rub your cum all over that hard cock. Fuck that's hot. Mmm...so creamy. I love to watch you cum. Thick ropes of hot, juicy sperm just for me. That's awesome. Look at you. You like it too, huh? I knew you would. Having a tight, young, eighteen year old girl watching you jerk off until you cum. Showing me all I need to know to please a man. I think I learned a whole lot here today.

Just let me catch my breath. I can still feel my pussy tingling and throbbing with excitement. Your cock is still pretty big, too. God, look at all that cum all over the place. I can smell it in the air. Can you smell my pussy? I love the smell of sex. Someone should make a candle that smells like that.

Here let me take my leg off of you and snuggle up to you. Come on, put your arm around my tight body.

Thank you so much for showing me how to please a man. I think the next time I touch a hard cock I'll be prepared to stroke it like a pro, just like you did today. Maybe I'll even come back and touch you. Would you like that? I think that can be arranged. I'll just come over one day and we'll have some fun. I'll touch you, and you can touch me. Who knows what will happen?

But really, thanks for jerking off for me. You're the best. I love your cock so much and tonight when I'm alone in my bedroom, under the covers, I'll be thinking about this while rubbing my pussy again. You do the same with your dick and maybe tomorrow I'll come back.

Let's just stay here like this for a while. Naked.

Here, I'll play with your cum and you can watch; maybe even fall asleep.

Until next time, baby...

ROOM SERVICE

It had been Lacey's idea.

"Let's get jobs at the beach this summer," she'd said. "We'll spend every spare minute we're not working laying in the sand, soaking up rays, flirting with hot surfers."

In theory, it had been a brilliant idea. Elena loved the beach and the sun and hot surfers... she could definitely use a few more of those in her life. And Lacey's big plan had worked out well...for Lacey. Lacey got hired to work one of the restaurants on the boardwalk. She spent her afternoons and days off basking in the sun alone, while Elena made beds, vacuumed and scrubbed toilets in the gorgeous Golden Galleon Hotel.

It paid well, and she could see and hear the ocean from the open balcony of every oceanfront room she had to clean, but the day was usually more than half-over before she finished work, and while the nightlife certainly left little to complain about, Elena had come for the sun and the sand and the surfers, not moonlit walks on the beach all alone. She tended to be a little on the shy side, and without her best friend prowling the club scene at her side, meeting anyone was practically out of the question.

And people were slobs. No one wanted to think about cleaning up after themselves on vacation, which was perfectly understandable, but not flushing the toilet after taking a shit was just plain lazy, not to mention disgusting. Holding her breath she pushed down the handle and stepped out of the bathroom to grab the air freshener from her cart. After spraying a healthy dose all over the room, she opened up the balcony to air out the room completely while she cleaned.

Most of the Golden Galleon's guests were upper-middle class families with bratty, spoiled children who liked to smear melted chocolate on the crisp white bedsheets, and leave rings of crusted sand and stinky shells soaking in the bathroom sinks. They rarely tipped well, despite the messes they left behind when checking out, and most of them talked to her like she didn't speak English, which was just insulting.

But she did her job, neatly tucking the corners on every freshly made bed, hanging clean white towels from the racks and even folding the hand towels in the bathroom into elegant swans before replacing all the complimentary toiletries. She emptied out the trashcans and always walked through each room one last time to make sure she didn't miss anything before closing up the balcony and moving onto the next room without a do-not-disturb sign hanging from the knob.

She smiled sweetly at every guest she passed in the hallway, saying good morning and even sharing conversation with those who weren't too stuck up to be friendly. She supposed it wasn't all that bad, but she'd come to the beach for the sun and the sand and the surfers, and spending her days locked up inside the Golden Galleon while everyone else in the world was spending their vacation actually vacationing was a little depressing.

Arriving at room 3406, she knocked twice and called out, "Housekeeping," listening for a response from within. After a few seconds with no answer, she knocked again, waited and then slid her keycard into the slot. She turned the knob, pushing open the door with her backside while gathering a stack of fresh sheets from her cart. She popped in her earbuds, pressed play on her iPod and went to work stripping the comforter from the queen-sized bed nearest the door.

She was tugging off the sheets when something rolled out of the bed and bounced across the floor before disappearing under it when she yanked the dirty sheets away. With a curse and a sigh, Elena dropped to her knees to search for whatever it was with a blind hand beneath. Scooting along the edge of the bed with her ass up in the air, she tilted her head down but her own shadow obscured the dark space no matter which way she turned.

"Shit," she muttered, flattening her body to stretch her arm further into the darkness. "Oh, come on," she groaned. At last, her fingertips stretched across the round, rubber curve and whatever it was rolled toward her. Grabbing it in her hand, she drew it out, crawling backwards across the floor and nearly screaming when she felt cool, damp skin against the backs of her bare thighs.

"Oh my god!" she shrieked, yanking the earbuds from her ears and turning a quick head back over her shoulder. "Oh my god, I am so sorry."

He was standing in a towel and nothing more, droplets of water rolling down his chest and across the tight muscles of his stomach. They clung and glistened in the soft patch of golden hair over his sculpted pectorals. Beads dripped from the damp, tousled locks of his blond hair. He was tall, pushing close to six foot six, she surmised, and every inch of him was lean muscle.

Elena scrambled to her feet, tugging down the hem of her uniform with her free hand and backing toward the door. She nearly stumbled over her own feet and banged her funny bone on the door handle in the process, trying desperately to hide the agonizing pain coursing down the length of her arm.

"I knocked but no one answered, and I didn't hear the shower."

"I was taking a bath, actually," he explained with a devilish grin that drew attention to the adorable cleft in his strong chin. "And listening to Stenhammar. I didn't hear you knock."

"I'm so sorry." She felt flustered, even more so when she glanced down at her hands and realized the object she'd retrieved from under the bed was a dildo. A big, thick, veiny cock that—were she in a comedy—would surely have wilted in her hand to add insult to injury. It was all she could do to keep from shrieking again. "So, so sorry. I—I didn't mean to disturb you. I'll just come back in a few hours."

"You're already here and the sheets have been torn from the bed." He shrugged and walked toward the balcony, drawing back the drapes and pushing open the doors to let the salted ocean breeze into the room. Hands perched on his hips as he stretched his neck and gazed out at the rolling waves, he added, "You might as well finish what you've started."

"Oh no, I couldn't. I shouldn't bother you," she protested. "I'll leave you and come back to finish up after you've gone to the beach."

"Honestly, I insist." Drawing in a deep breath of that sweet air, he turned back to face her as he exhaled. "Please, finish your work."

"I couldn't, really. I'll just come back later."

"It's all right, Elena," he assured her, then asked, "that is your name, right? Elena? That's what the little card on the bedside table said."

"Yes." She swallowed hard. Was he taking note of her name so he could report her indiscretion to the concierge? That's what she would have done if it had been her in his shoes. Only he wasn't wearing shoes, she realized, eyes traveling down the length of his legs to his bare feet on the floor. His toes curled and dug into the carpet before flexing straight again. He had beautiful feet. Long, perfect toes and neatly trimmed nails.

"You just go back to what you were doing, Elena," he instructed. "And pretend I'm not even here. I'll try to stay out of your way."

As much as she hated wasting her summer cleaning up after other people on vacation, she needed that job.

Looking around the room, it was surprisingly clean already, but then he'd only just arrived the day before. She hadn't seen him check in, but she knew for a fact his room had been empty yesterday. "It won't take long. I'll just make up your bed and clean in the bathroom real quick and then I'll be out of your hair."

"Take your time." He stalked toward her, the towel that hugged his waist firmly knotted in place even as he walked. She realized she was still holding that dildo in her hand. God, she felt ridiculous and so humiliated she was sure that she would melt into a puddle on the floor any minute. But he seemed insistent that she go about her business. He held out his hand and smiled at her again, his amusement reaching his bright blue eyes as he curled his fingers around the bulging head of the toy and gently jerked it from her grasp. "I do believe this belongs to me."

Elena swallowed again and let it go, avoiding the intensity of his gaze. He was taking great pleasure in her discomfort, she could feel it, and when he moved passed her and back into the bathroom, she swore she thought she heard him chuckle softly to himself just before the water in the sink began to run.

She finished tearing the sheets from the bed with trembling hands, her heart racing so fast inside her chest she was starting to feel lightheaded. And her face was on fire; she could only imagine how red it was, splotchy embarrassment spreading down her cheeks and neck. She'd worked at the hotel three weeks and had taken great pride in the fact that she'd never walked into a room while it was still occupied. Some of the other girls on staff told horror stories about walking in on couples in the middle of sex, while even others still had mentioned catching a few strangers jerking off. At least he'd only been bathing, she thought, though that did less to comfort and assuage her embarrassment than she'd hoped it might.

Why did he have to be so attractive? Had it been some middle-aged, bald and pot-bellied, lobster-red business man burnt by the sun it would have been easy to just veil her eyes and walk away, but this guy was gorgeous. And confident too. There was nothing in the world sexier than confidence.

"Are you a local?" he asked on his way out of the bathroom.

"No, sir," she replied, returning her attention to the bedsheets. "My best friend and I came down here to work for summer break."

"A college student," he surmised. "Where are you from?"

"Pittsburgh," she replied, hiking up the left corner of the mattress and sweeping the sheet underneath before dropping it back down.

"What do you study there?"

"Photography."

"An artist," he mused. "Very nice. I imagine you've taken some pretty impressive photographs here at the beach."

"Sunsets, mostly," she replied, shimmying down the edge of the bed while tucking in the slack. "I don't get out much during peak daylight hours."

"That's too bad." He took a seat in the chair near the open balcony, still wearing nothing but a towel. "The sunrises here are just as stunning as the sunsets. In fact, probably even more so."

Elena tried to focus on her work, but with that towel-clad god in the room it was downright impossible. Spreading the comforter over the sheets, she arranged and tucked the pillows before smoothing out the edges and stepping back to admire her work.

He'd watched the entire act, fingers steepled beneath his cleft chin, eyes shining with interest. When she bent to gather the crumpled, dirty sheets from the end of the bed, she swore she saw him tilt his head to get a better look at her ass just before she stood up.

"I never understood the concept of a made bed," he admitted, straightening in the chair. "You're just going to sleep in it again, so why go to all the trouble."

"Here at the Golden Galleon, we want your stay to be comfortable. That means fresh, clean sheets every morning, unless you request otherwise."

"I see," he nodded. "And I do appreciate the

effort."

Elena opened the door and stuffed the dirty sheets into the laundry bag on the side of her cart. She gathered new bottles of shampoo and tiny soaps, stacking them atop fresh towels before backing into the room again.

"I'm just going to clean up in your bathroom real quick, and then I'll leave you."

"Don't feel you have to hurry on my account," he said. "I'm actually enjoying this, though I think I'd enjoy watching much more if you were naked."

Surely, she hadn't heard him properly. Had he just said he would enjoy watching her clean his room naked? Elena didn't know what to say, if she should say anything at all, so she avoided that intense gaze of his and nudged her way into the bathroom.

Steam still dripped down the wide, full-length mirror, but even through the haze she could see the pink flush of her cheeks. The dildo was propped upright on the vanity, it's thick, veiny beauty almost mocking her as she worked around it. After wiping down the sink, she gathered up the old bottle of shampoo and dumped the opened soap into the trash, replacing them with fresh samples. She spritzed glass-cleaner across the mirror and lifting onto the tips of her toes, she swiped her busy hand over the surface until it was clear again.

He was lingering the doorway behind her, watching her work with almost predatory eyes. Stifling her startled gasp when she caught sight of him, Elena turned to face him, wide brown eyes searching his face, crumpled paper towels trembling in her grip.

"I'm almost finished." She didn't know what else to say.

"That's a shame." He shook his head and took a step toward her, the long fingers on his left hand lifting to caress her cheek. As they dropped down the length of her face, Elena shivered, the heat of her nervousness combining with the chills moving through her in delightful conflict. "As I said, I'm enjoying this a great deal."

Despite her discomfort, she was enjoying it too. For the first time since she'd taken that job she wasn't thinking about hurrying through her day to get outside before all the good rays of sun had been soaked in. His attention made her feel sexy, and even if she did tend to be a little on the shy side, her mind kept spiraling back to what he'd said a few minutes earlier about watching her clean his room naked.

She hadn't been with a guy in a few months, since February, actually and that hadn't been anything to write home about, but what about the woman he'd obviously used that dildo on? Was there a busty, blonde Mrs. Supermodel running around the Golden Galleon? Perhaps on a coffee run? Would she come bursting through the doors any minute and put a stop to this strange voyeuristic charade and make Elena feel less than inferior in her presence?

"A beauty like you should be out on the beach," he told her, lifting her chin so she had no choice but to look into those incredible blue eyes. "In nothing but that beautiful skin."

He lowered his mouth across hers as he

whispered those words, soft, moist lips hardening into an aggressive kiss that caught her off guard even though she'd seen it coming. He was so close she could smell the body wash and shampoo he'd used in the bathtub, feel the dampness of his towel and the hard rise of his excitement pressing out to greet her. She stiffened a little, her mind screaming *kiss him back you stupid fool*, but her body refused to react.

"I'm making you nervous," he observed, still hovering over her. His long fingers curled around her shoulder as he leaned back to look at her, intense gaze still gripping her.

"A little bit," she murmured softly.

"Loosen up, Elena." There was an edge of dominance in his voice that made her shiver, the flames of desire rising until she could literally feel them burning in her belly. Just standing there with him that way was making her wet, the white cotton of her panties clinging to the lips of her cunt when she shifted her feet in an attempt to follow his order. "Relax."

"I... I should finish my work."

Was she stupid? It was the most interesting thing that had happened to her since she'd taken that job, and she was trying to weasel out of it like a little chicken?

She watched the left corner of his mouth rise into a devious grin. Even if she was going to play the part of the chicken, he seemed to have every intention of assuming his role as the big bad wolf. His hard mouth came down on hers again, crushing her lips in dominance and stumbling her back two steps. She could feel the hard press of the sink against the small of her back, but that bit of support only seemed to encourage him. Hands slid down her arms and around her back, over the curve of her ass with fingers squeezing until he gripped the backs of her thighs and hiked her upward to sit on the vanity top.

"I'm your work now," he told her. "And I've been a very dirty boy."

Elena gulped, eyes fluttering closed as she tilted her head back and delighted in the firm press of his hands down the front of her thighs. He gripped and slid her skirt and apron upward, fingertips kneading into the flesh before pushing the bunched up fabric around her waist and stepping back to have a look at her. He nudged her legs apart with his hands, inspecting the damp crotch of her panties and smiling again.

She was so wet and turned on, it was almost embarrassing, but he didn't seem to mind. He rolled the tip of his finger over the wet cotton, tickling devilishly until she started to squirm.

"Like that, do you?" He almost seemed to smirk when he asked that. "I know something you'll like even better."

The erection that had risen behind his towel was impossible to ignore, and when he caught her heavily-lidded gaze surveying the bulge there, he leaned forward and rubbed his toweled cock against her panties. It felt huge and thick, though that could have just been the illusion of the towel. Even still, she did like the way it felt, that rough cloth brushing through the throbbing, cotton-clad layers between her legs.

Reaching for the tuck near his hip, Elena boldly

tugged the towel away and he stepped back a little to let it fall, his long cock bouncing back up as if to say hello. She couldn't take her eyes off of it, her intrigue rising to gasping levels as her heart raced and fluttered inside her. She'd never done anything so daring before, and the excitement that came with this stranger was almost more than she could stand. She didn't even know his name and yet she wanted him inside her. Even though she was scared, she wanted to let herself go and completely experience this rare moment of promiscuity she had done almost nothing to initiate.

He gripped his cock in his hand and stepped toward her again, rubbing the smooth, bulging head against her panties. "You like that?" he asked. "Does it feel good?"

"Mm," she breathed out that one syllable.

"You want it inside it you, don't you?"

She watched him tease, eyed the careful way he circled those long fingers around his dick and brushed it up and down her unexposed cunt. Occasionally he stroked his own length, the act itself turning her on more than the feel of his hard head bouncing against that thin wall of fabric keeping them apart. He had a beautiful cock, long, straight and slender and bulging with thick purple veins. She tentatively reached out to touch it, brushing along the smooth skin and making him shiver just a little.

"Stroke it," that gruff whisper was a two word command she couldn't resist.

Fingers curling around his shaft, she drew them gently along the length, lowering again and again and watching his face. He tilted his head back and to the side, eyes fluttering closed, the tip of his tongue moistening the dry skin of his lips.

"Yeah," he encouraged her. "Oh yeah, just like that. Stroke it."

Continuing the slow and steady pressure of her grip on his cock, every time he moaned or whispered she felt herself getting wetter, hotter, more eager for him, but the fact that he'd taken the initiative to make her summer worth celebrating made her want to please him all the more. She scooted off the edge of the counter and knelt on the cold tiled floor in front of him. He towered over her, head tilted down, approval flashing across his lips.

Elena darted her tongue out first to taste him, flickering teasingly across his head and forcing a throaty groan of appreciation from him. She swirled her tongue around the bulging mushroom, dancing it over his hole and then she closed her lips around his cock and began to gently suck him deeper into her mouth. She stroked and licked down the length, the moisture of her drooling saliva making every glide of her hand smoother and more precise.

She felt his hand on the back of her head, pressing down gently as his hips surged forward in an escalating rhythm. He was fucking her mouth, pushing so deep between her lips she actually thought she might gag a few times, but she kept going. Quickening the tug and pull of her hand, she bobbed up and down his length, occasionally swirling her tongue around his pole until she came to the cool sack dangling beneath. She sucked his balls, gripping them in her hand and gently squeezing before lapping her hungry tongue all the way to his head again. He jerked his hips forward with a delighted gasp as he forced himself so far into her mouth she actually did gag a little. The tense squeeze of her throat muscles only served to draw him in deeper, but she backed off and he pulled out of her mouth.

He grabbed her by the chin and pulled her to her feet again. Her skirt and apron had fallen down, but he wrenched them up again quickly and tugged her panties down so fast she thought she heard them tear. She wriggled them down the length of her legs and then stepped out of them, leaving them on the floor when he hoisted her back up onto the counter and dropped down to inspect what she had to offer.

The hot pulse of his exhaled breath across her slick, dripping pussy made her shudder, but not near as badly as she shivered when he brought two curious fingers up to spread her throbbing lips apart. When he brushed his thumb across her clit, chills shuddered through her and she squirmed, much to his grinning delight. She was absolutely dripping, his fingers gliding through her slit with ease and poking into her tight hole.

Elena's hips pushed forward almost on instinct, her hungry cunt devouring both fingers to the knuckles. He laughed and lifted his gaze to watch her face, sliding those fingers in and out of her while stroking his thumb across her clit. He leaned forward, tongue darting out to flicker between thumb-strokes and causing her to gasp with surprised delight.

She hadn't been with a lot of guys, and certainly none who'd ever done that. She'd seen it in pornos before, had daydreamed about it while fluttering a gentle finger over her own sensitive nub in the shower, but her imagination was nothing compared to the reality of a warm, slippery tongue and soft lips swirling and kissing and suckling the most sensitive part of her body.

"Ooh," she cooed, catching a glimpse of his raised eye again. He didn't stop what he was doing, but wanted to let her know the sounds of her excitement were encouraging.

She watched his long pink tongue sweep through her folds, dipping in low before sliding up to titillate her pulsing nub. "Oh yes," she gasped when he pushed both fingers in a little harder, stretching them through her clenched walls. He tempered the stroke of his fingers with the fast, tender lash of his tongue in a perfect rhythm that made her whine and moan, sounds she tried to bury in her shoulder. His lips sucked in her, drawing her into his mouth, between the gentle bite of his nibbling teeth.

"Oh god, that feels so good," she whispered. "So good."

"You taste divine," he told her before diving in deeper and deeper, the tip of his nose brushing across her clit when he stretched the length of his tongue into her depths.

It came on so quick, she almost didn't realize she was about to come. The only orgasms she'd ever had came from the curious explorations of her own fingers and the vibrating massager she kept neatly tucked away in a drawstring bag beside her bed. But the orgasm brought on by the attention he was paying her just then was more intense and wonderful than any she'd ever had before. As soon as she started to shiver and moan, he drew his fingers out and dropped down to lap at the gushing flood of excitement. It was all she could do to keep herself from screaming with delight, every muscle in her body tightening against that trembling wave of absolute bliss as she came.

She surprised herself, grasping onto the short locks of his mussed blonde hair and gripping tight, pushing him closer, ramming her cunt against his mouth. It was the most perfect and wonderful feeling she'd ever felt and she never wanted it to stop. He seemed only too happy to oblige, jamming his fingers into her slippery hole and ramming them in hard, quick pulses again.

It took much longer to bring her back around to orgasm, but the second was even more intense than the first, her entire body stiff and rigid with anticipation and then turning to absolute jelly when she finally released. Laughing at the rising pant of her heaving chest when he drew back, once more he raised those devilish blue eyes to meet hers. Licking his lips as he pushed to his full height, the countertop brought her wide open legs in perfect proximity to his hard, eager cock.

He stepped closer to her, gripping himself with one hand and guiding it toward her wet and waiting hole. He teased her at first, swirling and sliding just his head through her puffy pink lips, lingering at the edge of her opening then poking inside before drawing out again. Elena cried out, desperate for all of him, every last inch of him inside her.

He was so much taller than her that he had to lean down to whisper, "What do you want?" The heat of his breath sent shivers through her, and she could smell the musty scent of her own pussy on his skin, its stickiness brushing against her face when his tongue darted out to tickle her ear. He drew the lobe between his teeth, biting, sucking, whispering, "Do you want me to fuck you?"

Something about that crass suggestion only intensified her need for him. The husky sound of his voice, the suggestive tone in his words. "Yes." She ached for him, felt like she would die if she didn't feel his cock inside her.

"Say it," he commanded. "Tell me what you want me to do."

"Fuck me," she pleaded.

He went on teasing her, pushing in to give her just a little taste, then drawing out completely just to hear her whimper. "You didn't say please."

She'd never wanted anything more in her life than she wanted to feel him inside her right then. "Please," she cried, "fuck me."

Before she'd even finished saying the words he slammed into her hard and she wailed excitement, the bare cheeks of her ass sliding back from the sheer force of his thrust. She gripped the edges of the marble counter to hold herself in place, providing a stable slamming board for the heavy hammer of his hips against hers. His length moved through her, pounding into her depths until every breath that left her was a desperate, eager gasp of surprise. Surprise that it felt so good to get fucked so hard. Surprise that she was actually letting a total stranger fuck her while she was on the job. She could get fired for what she was doing, but she didn't care. There was no turning back now and it felt too good to stop.

His arm came around her, swept up her spine until his fingers tangled into the hair of her dangling ponytail. He gripped it and tugged down, exposing the flesh of her neck for his lips and tongue, his teeth. Every suckling nip made her shudder and writhe against him, the soft mewling sounds she made urging him on.

The wet sound of his cock pounding in and out of her pussy was delicious and as it mingled with their rising moans of pleasure, Elena thought again about the dildo she'd found in the bed. Was there another woman, she wondered? Would she come barging through the door at any moment, her vacation ruined by the sight of her husband or boyfriend or whatever he was banging away at another woman? It shouldn't have, but the thought of getting caught heightened her pleasure, making her buck her hips faster to swallow him inside her cunt over and over again.

"You like that?" he purred like a cat, his wet lips trailing across her cheek, tongue slipping out to tease at her lips before she opened her mouth to his hungry kiss.

"Yes," she whimpered. "Yes!"

Their tongues tangled and their bodies danced to the repetitive chorus of grunting moans and fevered whispers that sent shivers rolling across the surface of her flesh. She'd never been a bad girl before, never taken the kind of risk she was taking right then, but in the heat of the moment, she didn't care.

"You feel so good," he said. "So tight and wet."

"Fuck me harder," she begged. "Fuck me so hard it hurts."

The heavy bones of his hips crashed against hers, his long cock pumping in and out of her so hard, she could feel the early tingling of release again. She'd never had an orgasm during sex, but the promise of it lingered behind the force of every thrust of his shaft through her walls.

He grunted with every slam, making her yelp a few times, but she didn't care.

Outside in the room, she could hear the distant roll of the ocean, smell the clean brisk scent of it on the breeze rustling through the sheer drapes across the open porch. She wondered how many people on the beach could hear him fucking her and she didn't care about that either. She was in heaven, five pumps away from the only orgasm she'd ever had with a cock inside her. It was building up, rising, the tight muscles of her stomach rippling almost in protest and then she came.

She wrapped her legs around him to hold him still while she clenched and squealed, every muscle inside her soft and then tight, tight and then soft again almost completely against her will. He continued to jerk his hips slowly forward, still stoking the fire of her release. The soft cool sack beneath his cock slapped gently at the fold of skin between her cunt and her ass, almost tickling each time he slipped inside her.

When she loosened her legs he started to furiously pump in and out of her again. He worked himself hard, the wet slap of their sweaty skin almost painful, but it felt good, even as her excitement began to ebb away.

He closed his eyes and rested his forehead against hers, rutting her good and hard until he couldn't hold back anymore.

"I'm cumming," he told her. "Here it comes."

Stepping back, he tugged his cock from the tight squeeze of her muscles and gripped it in one hand, still pumping the length of his shaft. It shined and gleamed with her juices, and though she'd never actually watched anything like it before, Elena took pleasure in watching him stroke his own cock. His grip was confident and his confidence was the sexiest thing about him. Harder, faster, he knew exactly what he was doing and that was sexy too.

She giggled with delight when a few seconds later, white hot spurts of cum jetted from the swollen purple head, squirting in streams across the tops of her thighs and immediately cooling as the droplets rolled down her skin. She watched the last few spurts shoot out to catch her knee, and he laughed a little to as he caught his breath and allowed the already softening tool in his hand to drop and dangle heavy and still half-hard between his legs.

"I should let you get back to work," he said. For a moment, he just stood there in front of her and then he knelt to grab his towel, tying it around his waist again and walking out of the bathroom.

Elena sat on the countertop trying to wrap her head around what she'd just done. There was a niggling twinge of guilt on her conscience when she finally dropped down and grabbed the clean towels she'd brought in with her to wipe the cum from her thighs. She wriggled back into her panties and glanced out into the room. He was standing in front of the open balcony again, hands on his hips as he watched the gulls swoop down into the ocean just outside the door.

It wasn't easy, but she forced herself to get back to work. She sprayed and wiped down the vanity again, her gaze resting over the dildo still standing tall near the corner. She never did find out who it had belonged to, whether or not there was a wife or girlfriend with him. She cleaned out the shower and scrubbed the toilet before quickly sweeping the bathroom floor. She replaced the towels she'd used from the stash on her cart and then gave the room a quick once over before resting her eyes on the man who'd just fucked her silly while on the clock.

"If you need anything else, just call the concierge."

"What time do you finish work?" he asked.

"Five o'clock."

"Good. I may need more towels later." He glanced back over his shoulder at her, that sly grin playing on his lips once more. "Say around three-thirty?"

Elena smiled and reached for the handle on the door. "I'll be happy to bring you more towels at three-thirty, Mr..."

"Birkeland," he replied. "Xander Birkeland."

"All right, Mr. Birkeland," she nodded, tugging open the door. "I'll see you then."

As she closed the door to room 3406 and

stepped up to her cart in the hallway, she felt a strange mixture between giddiness and guilt. If anyone ever found what she'd done in there, she'd be fired in an instant, but she wouldn't take it back if given the option to do it over again. It had felt too good, every last inch of him. She couldn't wait to tell Lacey all about it; her best friend would be green with envy.

Maybe, she thought, pushing her cart up the hallway, past the doors with do-not-disturb signs dangling from their handles, spending her summer indoors at the Golden Galleon wasn't going to be so bad after all.

She stopped in front of room 3412, leaning in to knock before calling out, "Housekeeping."

THE LUCKY ONE

I'm a fairly easygoing guy who believes that you should treat people the way you would like to be treated. That's not to say that I'll commiserate over everyone I see who's in trouble, but you can best be sure that I'll take a good look at the situation before I make a decision. My wife says I'm too nice; that it's my Achilles heel. Maybe she's right, but in this crazy, messed up world, we need a few nice guys every now and again to remind us that we're all part of the same race. The human race.

Another problem I have, and one I freely admit to, is saying no. Someone wants something done? I'm there. Whether it's helping a friend move, driving them to the airport, or providing a little financial support every so often, they can always count on me. Sometimes it can be a burden, and make me feel like I have too much on my plate, but most times it's just my way of being polite. It's not that I don't like saying no; I have on many an occasion. It's just that we're all in this together, so why not try and help each other out when we can?

Of course, I never expected that my generosity and empathetic nature would eventually land me in one of the tightest spaces I'd ever been in my life, but it was bound to happen one of these days I guess. And when I say *tight spaces*, I mean tight spaces. Not your average, caught-between-a-rock-and-a-hard-place space, but a really, tight space. One that leaves you feeling conflicted, confused, and downright awful about the way you do things. Yes, my good nature came back to bite me in the ass, but that doesn't mean I've lost hope in my fellow man, or myself. On the contrary. I've found new hope in the world, and in the way I do things. To say I feel rejuvenated wouldn't be that far off. Truth is, we all slip and fall along the way, and that's what happened to me, but that doesn't mean I can't find the good in a bad situation, right? In this case, there was a lot of good to go around, and it's something that I'll never forget.

It all started on a hot summer night. The kind of night where you can feel the heat hanging in the air like a thick coat of honey. You move slower, think slower, and when you take a breath it feels like your chest might cave in because it's so damn humid. The air conditioning wasn't working in the car so I had all the windows down, but even then all that did was blow hot air around me like a swirling tornado of heat, with me in the eye of the storm.

Despite all that, though, I was still feeling pretty good. I own a small business, selling used books and comics, the likes of which can be very rare at times. I had just gotten off one of the best sales days I'd ever had, raking in over seven grand at the shop due in part to this guy who came in and bought a Fantastic Four #1 that had been sitting on the shelf for quite some time. He walked away happy, and I walked away with a fatter wallet, so it was a good deal for both of us. I cranked the stereo in the car and listened to Tom Petty, which in my opinion is some perfect driving music.

I still had about another twenty miles to go before I reached home, which is a small country house in Pennsylvania that's off the beaten path. A nice, quiet place that the wife and I just adore. It's a two-story, three bedroom, one-and-a-half-bath place that we've lived in for the better part of ten years now. I grew up a city boy, but when Janice and I got married she wanted to live in the country. Best decision I succumbed to, really. The air is cleaner, the stars are brighter at night, and the neighbors are as pleasant as a deep tissue massage. Not to mention the wildlife. I had never seen a deer up close before I moved to the middle of nowhere, now I see them almost everyday when I check the mail.

So there I was, hotter than hell and on top of the world, when I see this car up ahead on the side of the road. Its four-ways are flashing and the trunk is up, and there's someone leaning into it like they're rummaging around for something. I had two choices here. I could either let it go and keep driving, or slow down and stop to see what the trouble was. I wasn't so much worried about a crime taking place. In my neck of the woods crime is almost non-existent. It was more the time constraint that was cause for concern. Janice was home waiting up for me with a bottle of wine and a fresh apple pie to celebrate the day's sales. I didn't want to disappoint her.

As my headlights flooded the scene, though, I saw that the driver of the vehicle was a young lady. There was no mistaking that. Her ass was stuck up in the air waving back and forth like a white flag of surrender, beckoning me over for help. Her legs were as long as a Texas sky, and they came up to a pair of tight jean shorts. Her skin glistened with sweat, and it was that sexy sheen that did me in. How could any man resist that?

I slowed down my car and pulled off the road right behind her. My tires crunched gravel and I turned down the stereo, not wanting to startle her. She turned around and stood up, shielding her eyes with one hand to block out the glare of my headlights. I turned them off but left the car running, unfastened my seat belt and stepped out into the night.

"Having some trouble?" I called.

"Flat tire," she said.

I walked up to her and saw that those long legs were attached to one of the most succulent upper bodies I had ever seen in my life. The girl was wearing a tight, white tank top that barely covered her flat stomach, and like her legs, the rest of her was drenched in sweat as well. You could smell it in the air mixed with her perfume, which had the aroma of a strawberry milkshake. Her chest heaved underneath the tight material, sticking to her like taffy. She wasn't wearing a bra and I could trace the outline of her areola as her nipples poked out to greet me. I did my best not to stare, and turned my attention to her face to take the edge off.

She was gorgeous. Her unblemished cheeks were smooth and silky, giving way to a tiny chin and long neck. Her nose curled up in the air and beneath it, thin, ruby red lips smiled back at me. Her face was surrounded by wavy, chestnut hair that danced in the breeze, taking my breath away for a split second. I looked at her back tire and sure enough, it was flatter than a penny crushed by a train.

I nodded at it for a moment and once I trusted myself enough to speak without my voice cracking, I said, "Got a spare?"

She shook her head. Of course she didn't.

"Huh," was all I could think to say. She was in quite the pickle and I didn't know if I could help her. I didn't have a spare myself, or a jack. It's a shame, too, because I really wanted to stay and lend her a hand.

Not one to give up, I stood there for a moment, staring from the tire to her, as she looked on, waiting for me to help her like I was a knight in shining armor instead of just a guy in a pair of blue jeans, runners, and a t-shirt.

"You call anyone?"

"Phone's dead," she said.

I reached into my pocket and fished out my iPhone, and handed it to her. She hesitated, but eventually reached for it. Our fingers brushed one another for the briefest of moments, sending a tingle down my side and between my legs. Skin so soft you'd swear it was made from cotton, that's what it was like.

"Thanks," she grinned, noticing my googly eyes.

What did she expect? She was practically naked in front of me. Not that I was thinking of doing anything to her, but she was drop dead stunning. Couldn't have been more than nineteen, either. Lord, if I was ten years younger, but alas, I was thirty-three and married. I reached down and played with my wedding ring, too, just to remind myself, while she turned her back and made a call.

Try as I might though, I couldn't avoid staring at that ass of hers. So tight and round, and her shorts were short enough to show off part of her cheeks as well. I felt the bulge in my pants begin to grow, and I shifted from one foot to the other, looking back at my car to distract myself.

Her voice was high-pitched but not squeaky-annoying like some girls' are. I listened as she spoke, giving directions to where we were as best she could. She turned around and looked at me once, smiling and rolling her eyes. I smiled back, my eyes instinctively flickering to her breasts. She winked at me and turned back around, shutting her trunk. After a few more minutes she got off the cell and handed it back to me. I gladly took it and shoved it back in my pocket, hoping that it would mask the chub I was still experiencing.

"Ugh," she moaned. "I hate this."

"Problem?"

"No. I don't know. Roadside assistance is going to come and help, but they can't be here for like, an hour."

"Ah, man. That sucks," I replied.

"Yeah."

We both stood our ground, looking at one another for a while, neither of us giving an inch. I knew Janice was at home waiting for me, but this girl was in trouble. I couldn't just leave her there, could I? Alone, in the middle of nowhere? What if someone who wasn't so nice came along and tried something and I heard about it on the news the next day? I'd feel awful knowing that I could have prevented that. Sure, there's not a lot of crime, but all it takes is just one person with bad intentions to ruin everything. Did I want to risk it, or leave her high and dry?

I shuffled my feet from side to side again, feeling a little awkward, when she spoke up.

"Listen, I know you don't have to, but do you think that you could hang out here with me until they show up?"

There. I had the perfect opening to stay, but my conscience got the better of me. Thinking of Janice, sitting in the living room in front of the television, wondering where I was. I couldn't do that to her, as much as I wanted to stay and console this pretty young thing, my wife came first.

"I'd love to," I said, "but I got someone at home waiting for me."

She pouted and took me by the hand, drawing me closer to her like I was on a string. Looking up into my eyes, she batted her lashes and crossed her knees like an innocent teenager, only this girl was far from innocent. She knew exactly what she was doing, and I let her guide me toward her beautiful body.

"Please?" she whined. "You've been so helpful already. I promise I'll make it up to you."

I stared into her eyes, searching them for some semblance of understanding. A last ditch effort to make her see things my way, but all she cared about was that I waited with her. And what of this promise? Did that mean what I think it meant, or was she just being a tease? Using her sexuality to get what she wanted? I used to see that a lot in the city, but not so much out here in the country.

Still, she was alone, with no one but me to help her. Janice would understand that, and as long as I kept my hands to myself, we'd be okay.

"Just a second," I said, turning my back and dialing home. I caught a brief glimpse of a smile before she was out of view.

"Hello?" Janice answered.

"Hi, honey. It's me."

"Everything okay?" she asked, already a hint of concern to her voice.

"Oh, yeah. It's fine, but there's this girl stuck out on the road with a flat tire. I stopped to help her but she doesn't have a spare so I let her use my phone to call assistance, but they won't be here for an hour. I know we had plans but do you mind if we postpone them for an hour? She's all alone and I don't want her waiting here all by herself at night."

There was a long, drawn out sigh on the other end of the line, like an inflatable raft letting out air. Janice wasn't happy, but I hoped she understood.

"I'm sorry, babes," I added for emphasis.

She's put up with a lot over the time we've been married. My comic book obsession, my love of geek culture and toys, and I'm always going out of my way to help people and be nice to them, so sometimes that gets in the way of our plans. It hasn't happened in a while, but when it does and it affects her, Janice will brood better than any emo kid on the Internet.

She cleared her throat and I could hear her lips part, her tongue clacking against the roof of her mouth. "I guess," she finally said, "but I'm eating a piece of this pie without you."

"Deal. I'm sorry, baby. You know how I get."

"Yeah, yeah, I know. Don't worry about it. I'd do the same thing probably. Just, hurry home, okay?"

"I will. Love you."

"I don't know why, but I love you too."

She hung up and I couldn't help but laugh. Janice is so dramatic sometimes, and it usually comes across in a comical way so that people don't take her too seriously. She just wanted to let me know that she wasn't mad, that's all.

I put my phone in my pocket and turned to face my damsel in distress. In those brief moments that I was talking to my wife, I nearly forgot how good she looked, but now that I was staring at her, it all came flooding back like a tidal wave assaulting my senses. Her scent, her appearance, the way her skin felt and the sound of her voice. All that was left was to...taste her.

I blinked once, twice, three times, a little harder than I should have. She giggled in my direction.

"Everything okay?" she asked.

"Yeah," I said, shaking my head. "I'll wait with you until roadside assistance gets here."

"Perfect. Thank you so much."

Her eyes did betray a great deal of gratitude, which made me feel better. She wasn't just playing some sort of game with me. She really did want help, and I had come to the rescue right in the nick of time. Lucky me.

I went back to my car and killed the engine, but left the stereo on low. She went around and opened the hood of her vehicle to let the tow-truck know that she was the one in peril, and then came around back where I was sitting on the hood of mine, facing her. She joined me, sitting on the warm metal just a couple of inches away from me.

"So what's your name?" I asked her, trying to instigate some small talk.

"Melody," she replied. "Yours?"

"Michael," I said.

Melody stuck out her hand, waiting for me to accept it. I did, without hesitation, and when our skin met for the second time that night, I became transfixed on her beauty and the way she oozed confidence, staring into her eyes like a man in a daze before allowing my gaze to linger up and down her body.

"You like what you see?" she asked.

I stood there, still gripping her palm, only now my jaw hung open a little. Melody wasn't shy, that much was for certain, but I was. Especially when asked such a direct question. Did I like what I saw? Of course I did, but I wasn't going to tell her that. Not with words, anyway. I didn't have to. My eyes said it all for me.

"It's okay," she continued, "I'm used to getting the attention."

She released me and I dropped my arm back to my side, still looking at her. I tried to find my voice, saying, "I'll bet," but it came out hoarse and low. I cleared the frog from my throat, rubbing my Adam's apple in the process. Melody laughed and tossed her hair over her shoulders. She pursed her lips and raised her eyebrows, eyeing me up and down just like I had done with her.

"So," she said, leaning into me. "How about that promise?"

"Promise?"

"For staying with me. I said I'd make it up to you."

Melody inched her way closer and closer until she was practically on top of me. I closed my eyes, thinking that there was no way I could do something like this, but then she reached down and cupped my crotch, giving it a tight squeeze and whispering in my ear, "I'd love to make it up to you."

I moaned softly and swallowed--hard. She inserted her tongue into my ear, making me weak in the knees and causing my entire body to tingle with excitement. I didn't remember the last time I had felt this good. The circuit board that was my brain was overheating, sending all the blood in my head rushing to my cock as Melody continued to massage it while sucking ever so gently on my earlobe.

"I know what you want," her voice reverberated in my face and I felt my cheeks flush red. As hot as the night was, it felt even hotter standing next to her, and I knew that there was no way I'd be able to resist what she was offering. I didn't even know if I wanted to.

Melody shifted her body, coming around in front of me. She still gripped my groin in the palm of her hand, and she pressed her tits against my chest. I felt her hard nipples just below mine, like two, tiny pebbles pressing into my skin. She ran her tongue across my neck and I raised my chin, giving her full access. My hands reached around for her ass and when they found it, it was like touching Heaven, if Heaven felt like two, firm volleyballs. When they were sated, they reached around front and slid up her too-short tank top, grabbing at the two mounds of flesh pressed against me. Melody separated herself just enough to let me get a handful, and I pinched her nipples between thumb and forefinger before massaging her tits over and over. Her lips never touched mine, though, but I could smell her lip-gloss, they were that close. Like the rest of her, it filled my nostrils with the aroma of strawberries, a scent that always drove me wild when applied on a beautiful woman.

"That feels nice," she whispered at me. "I told you I'd make it up to you."

Then, without warning, she scrunched down in front of me and began playing with my belt buckle. I gasped, sending out a breath of hot air to mix with the night's humidity. She didn't get down on her knees because of the gravel, but she was down there nonetheless, putting all her weight on the balls of her feet, unwrapping me like a Christmas present. When my belt buckle was loose, she undid the button, slid down the zipper, and yanked my jeans and boxers down to my knees in one, swift motion. Despite the heat, the air felt cool on my cock, which was already standing at attention like a good soldier would, swaying back and forth. Melody wasted no time. She gripped it in her hand like a microphone and began stroking it up and down. I looked down and saw her staring back up at me, her eyes wide with anticipation.

She grinned once, and took me in her mouth, making tiny sucking noises while her head bobbed, and her cheeks contracted and expanded. I didn't know what to do with my hands, which were resting comfortably on the hood of my car, so I brought them around and placed them on the back of her head, my fingers getting tangled like bubblegum in her hair. Her tank top was pulled up over her tits, and they bounced back and forth as she began sucking me harder and faster, loosing whatever inhibitions she had left.

Her lips felt so fucking good wrapped around me like that. They traveled up and down the length of my shaft, and her hand continued to stroke in unison with them. She popped me out of her mouth and licked it up and down before going lower and playing with my balls on her tongue, flicking it over them again and again. I could feel them getting coated in her saliva, and she massaged them in the palm of her hand as she took the tip of me back between her lips, sucking hard on it. The sensation was incredible, and I released my grip on her head and slammed my hands down on the hood, moaning loudly at the pleasure she was bringing me. She, in turn, moaned with a mouthful of cock, eager to please me as best she could.

"Suck it," I told her, "suck it harder." I didn't know where that came from, but it seemed like the right thing to say to such a naughty girl like her. Usually I kept quiet during the act of sex, limiting my noises to mere grunts and moans, but with Melody it felt different. Perhaps it was the situation? It felt like something you'd see in a movie, and it caused me to become someone else who I might not be otherwise. I liked it, and spoke again. "Yeah, that's it," I said when she obeyed my first command. "Keep sucking it."

She did, releasing her hands and running them up my chest. I took them in mine and watched as she blew me with nothing more than her mouth to guide her. Then I raised my head to the sky and looked up at the stars twinkling back me, thinking about how lucky I was to have stopped when I did.

As Melody continued to work me over, I felt my balls getting tighter and tighter. The pressure mounting in them. She felt so amazing and I wanted her to keep going, but I also wanted to taste her, and experience what it was like to be inside such a creature. "You better stop," I said, and almost immediately she withdrew me from between her lips and stroked me a few more times with one hand, while she looked up into my eyes and wiped away some saliva from her chin with the other.

She stood up and we switched positions, with her back to the hood of the car this time. She rested her firm ass on it and spread her legs wide, grabbing at my shirt collar and pulling me close. She arched her back and tilted her chin back while I kissed her neck and ran my tongue down to her breasts. I popped one nipple in my mouth, sucking it slowly, then switched to the other for good measure, paying careful attention to the goosebumps on her smooth skin. Melody took me by the head and smashed my face even further into her, and before I knew it was gasping for breath after nibbling and sucking on her perky tits.

From there I slid my tongue lower, swirling it around her navel while I played with the button on her jeans shorts. Her flesh tasted sweet, just like the sweat and strawberries I had been smelling all along. It was so tender and beautiful, and I only had a moment to wonder what her pussy was like before it was splayed out before me like an all-you-can-eat buffet. She placed her feet on the front bumper and I got down on my knees, my bunched-up jeans providing them comfort. Melody was completely shaved down there, and her sweet cunt beckoned to me like a love song. I licked my lips and parted hers with my thumbs, getting a close look at her young pink. She was already sopping wet and when I dove in, her juice instantly covered my mouth and chin.

As good as this girl smelled, she tasted even better. I don't know what was in her diet, but it was definitely working. I ran my tongue up and down her slit then stiffened it and poked it into her hole over and over before sliding it over her clit, flicking it back and forth across her sensitive bud. Melody let out a long, exasperated cry of pleasure, despite it sounding so angry. She was focused—intense—and begged me to keep licking her. I did not disappoint, and I lapped at her pussy like a thirsty animal before mashing my mouth against her and sliding my tongue in as far as it could go, my nose breathing in her scent like it was fresh baked bread. She writhed and squirmed under me, her body pressing against the hood of the car. I looked up and saw her chest heaving up and down, so I reached forward and cupped her breasts in my hands. She placed hers overtop of them, encouraging me to squeeze tighter, which I did, as I continued to taste the most elegant pussy I'd ever experienced.

I finally let go of Melody's tits after a minute or so, and reached one hand down between my legs to stroke myself while I fingered her with my free hand, slipping two, eager fingers into her and wiggling them around before ramming them in and out. She enjoyed the roughness of it all, pushing her groin down against them. My cock got rock hard and I stood up, anxious to be inside her.

I leaned over and kissed her chest while running the head of my dick up and down her slit, getting it slick with her juice.

"Fuck me," she moaned. "Fuck me hard."

I bit at her neck like a man possessed and began sliding into her, feeling her tight hole expand with every inch that went in until it was stretched as far as it would go. Her muscles clenched around me and she wrapped her legs around my back, locking her ankles together. I slid in as deep as I could go until I felt my balls touch her ass, then I pushed just a little more, the head of my cock spasming inside of her. She cried out with great fury, clawing at my back through the fabric of my t-shirt. I hoped to hell she didn't leave any marks.

"Fuck you feel good," I moaned, beginning to get a rhythm going, sliding the shaft in and out of her, thrusting harder each time.

"You like that tight pussy?" she moaned. "Fuck it, baby. Fuck me."

I pressed my palms against the hood of the vehicle and worked my hips back and forth, loving every single sensation of her pussy wrapped around my cock. She was so slick, so wet, and so tight. I hammered myself into her as hard as I could then, pounding away like a jackhammer as the car began rocking back and forth with us like it was a waterbed. It squeaked and groaned under our weight, but I didn't let up. I kept on fucking Melody as hard as I could, looking down at her succulent body and marveling as her tits bounced up and down. I leaned my weight on one hand and grabbed at one breast with the other, kneading it hard. My cock didn't let up, and I felt my balls slap against her again and again, getting wetter each time with her juicy honey.

Sweat clung to both of us like a second skin, and beads of it dripped down from my forehead onto her. The stench of sex filled my nostrils with its wonderful aroma as we stared into one another's eyes, lost in the moment. She grinned at me and snapped her teeth hungrily in my direction, her little nose twitching in the process.

Melody unlocked her ankles and without thinking, I withdrew from her pussy and grabbed her arm, hauling her off the hood and turning her around. She bent over and the ass that I was so desperately attracted to earlier was sticking up at me, naked, like a fleshy heart waiting to be loved. I took my cock in my hand and guided it into her slowly from behind until once again, I was balls deep in her cunt. I grabbed onto her hips and began thrusting in and out, watching as my dick disappeared and reappeared, coated thicker each time with the white residue of her cum. Our flesh slapped together and there was no give. Melody was pushed up against the car as far as she could go, and I began hammering away in short, hard bursts of energy that made her moan louder and louder with each pounding.

Soon enough, I lost all control and reached for her shoulders, pulling her back as I pushed forward. She raised her head and told me to pull her hair, so I did, bucking hard against her like she was a bronco to be tamed. I ground my teeth together and tried to think about something else to take my mind off the rising tide of pleasure in my cock, but it was hopeless. Melody felt too good, and her pussy was too wet for me to concentrate on anything else. My breathing became shorter and labored, and my chest heaved up and down with each suck of air. Melody, sensing my weakness, looked up over her shoulder and licked her lips.

"Are you gonna let me taste you?" she asked.

I nodded and reluctantly pulled out, taking a step back as she crouched down in front of me. Melody took my slick dick in her hand and began stroking it faster and faster, opening up her mouth and sticking out her tongue in preparation. I brushed her hair out of her eyes and watched as her lips wrapped around my head and she sucked, tasting herself before tasting me. To my surprise, she continued sucking, and I winced as the first wave of pressure was released and I exploded in her mouth. She moaned, and formed a tight seal around me as a second wave hit, and then a third, my cum oozing out of my cock and down her throat. She gladly gulped it back with wide eyes that smiled up at me, cupping my balls in her hand and massaging them softly with her fingers while my rod jerked and spasmed over her tongue. I hadn't cum that much in a long time, and it felt tremendous. When I was done, Melody opened her mouth and I saw some of it on her tongue. She quickly swallowed it and sucked on me some more, making sure that she got every last drop of me.

"So good," she said, licking up and down the shaft.

I breathed a heavy sigh of relief and she stood up, adjusting her top so that it covered her breasts once again. My pants were still around my ankles and I grabbed them, and my boxers, and pulled them up, covering my vulnerability. She reached for her shorts and did the same, though she continued to smile at me.

"Not bad, huh?" she asked.

I laughed and shook my head.

"Not bad at all," I said.

"Told you I'd make it up to you if you waited with me," she giggled.

I nodded, saying nothing. I checked my watch just as a set of headlights breached the corner and flooded our vehicles. The tow-truck was here.

"Well, there's my ride," Melody said. "Thanks again for staying."

"Not a problem," I said.

"You were great, really."

"You too," I smiled.

The truck pulled up beside us and the driver rolled down his window. "Someone got a flat?" he yelled over the roar of his engine.

Melody raised her hand. "That's me."

"Okay," he said, killing the motor and stepping out.

I started to walk away but managed to overhear a bit of their conversation. Melody thanked the man, and said she'd make it up to him for coming out so late to help her. I couldn't help but laugh as I got into my car and started her up. That guy had no idea what he was in for.

Passing them, I honked a good-bye and headed for home, where Janice was still waiting up for me. I thought about what I'd say, about how I'd act, but then I realized that I was fine. I didn't feel anything, other than an overwhelming sense of calm deep in the pit of my stomach. What had happened, happened. Sure, maybe I should have been stronger and resisted temptation, but I wasn't going to make excuses. I felt more alive than ever. Freer, for some reason, and that feeling coupled with the fantastic day I had had at the store was all I needed to present to my wife when I walked through the front door.

Soon enough, I did just that, and Janice hugged me tight.

"Ewe, you're sweaty," she commented.

"Have you been outside?" I asked. "It's hotter than hell tonight, and the air conditioning is broken in the car."

"Well, you can get it fixed this week now," she grinned, referring to the great sales day I had.

"You know it," I smiled, kissing her on the lips.

"Why don't you take a shower and we'll celebrate."

"Absolutely."

She walked back to the living room as I headed for the bathroom, already peeling off my clothes before I got there. I stood under the cool stream of water and breathed a sigh of relief as it soaked my skin, cooling it by several degrees. Of course, as soon as I got out I'd be sweating bullets again no doubt, but that was fine. It would be my sweat, and it wouldn't be mixed with someone else's.

I toweled off and walked naked back into the living room. Janice was there, laying on the couch with the bottle of wine and apple pie on the coffee table. I thought of Melody while I was in the shower, and that was enough to get me horny again, and I wanted to ravish my wife and show her that I loved her, because I did.

"My, my," she said, slipping out of her flannel shorts and t-shirt.

I sat on the sofa next to her and we kissed. She grabbed for my cock and started stroking it up and down with care.

"What's got into you?" she whispered.

"Just...had a good day," I said.

"Lucky me," she smiled. Then she took me in her mouth and I closed my eyes, thinking *no, I'm the lucky one.*

IMPURE THOUGHTS

I've always wanted to fuck my best friend's wife, but up until last month I'd never had the courage to do anything about it. I know, I know, it's my best friend and some things are off limits, but if you'd seen Tammy you'd want to fuck her too!

She is, without a doubt, the most beautiful woman I've ever laid eyes on. She's 5'4" with long, raven black hair, skin as smooth and soft as velvet, an ass that just begs to be touched, and tits that are just a little too big for her small frame, with nipples that always seem to be hard. Every time I see her they're always poking out from beneath the fabric of whatever she is wearing. It's amazing.

Not only is she stunningly gorgeous, but she's nice, too. She has an amazing, wide smile filled with pearly white teeth and sparkling blue eyes that laugh back at you when you say something funny. She's kind to others, always says please and thank you, and when you sneeze she's the first one to say, "Bless you." She just has a good heart, something that makes her even more attractive.

How a guy like my buddy Dale ever ended up with a woman like that is beyond me.

I mean, Dale's nice enough, but sometimes he can be a real jerk. Not just to me, but to Tammy, also. Especially when he's been drinking. Cheap insults, little jabs, and mean scowls are all a part of his forte when he's had a few beers in him, which has been all too often these days.

Which is why I broached the subject with Tammy a little over two months ago when Dale wasn't around. I wanted to make sure she was okay, because I really do care about her. She assured me that everything was fine, that Dale just gets in these moods sometimes, but she was handling it as best she could. I told her if she ever needed someone to talk to that I was there for her, and she smiled and thanked me, and then wrapped her arms tight around me for a big bear hug, which I gladly accepted, and perhaps held for a little bit longer than was considered normal. When I let go I glided my hands down her back and looked her in the eyes, holding her stare for a moment before blushing and letting go.

From that moment, things were different between Tammy and I.

It was like she knew I wanted her, and she enjoyed teasing me over it. She started doing things like leaning over in front of me to pick something up, making sure her cleavage was on display and always catching my eye in the process. She began touching me more when we were talking, like my arm or shoulder or the small of my back, and whenever we all sat at a table together she made sure to get the seat right next to mine and lean into me when talking so I could smell her intoxicating perfume.

It drove me nuts, but Tammy? She was having a great ol' time knowing that there was another man in her life who could pay her some attention, and believe me, I was definitely giving her all the attention she deserved.

The thing is, I had no idea if she wanted me as much as I wanted her, or if she was just having fun at my expense. It was all very confusing.

Then, about a month ago, I got my answer when I was walking home from the store one day with a bag full of groceries, and she pulled up beside me and offered to give me a ride home. Even though I only had a couple of blocks left to walk I gladly accepted, because any chance to spend time with Tammy and I was all over that.

She told me Dale was at work and she was just out doing some shopping, having a day to herself. I asked how things were going with Dale and she just sort of shrugged it off like she didn't really want to talk about it. That was fine by me. When we got to my house I asked if she wanted to come inside for a drink and just chill out and she said sure, and we went inside where the air conditioning cooled us off from the hot, August sun.

Tammy was dressed in a navy blue tight tank top and short, black shorts. Her hair hung down straight over freckled shoulders that gleamed with sweat, and when she took a seat at my kitchen table, my eyes immediately noticed her rock hard nipples poking through the fabric of her top, which—by the way—was showing a generous amount of cleavage.

I swallowed, looked away, and brought two bottles of beer out of the fridge for us to enjoy. I took a seat next to her, smelling the mixture of perfume and sweat emanating off her luscious body, and twisted off both caps before handing Tammy her drink.

"Thank you," she said, taking it from me.

We both sat there for a while, sipping our beers and not saying much. It felt kind of...awkward. With everything that had been going on between us as of late, I found myself not really knowing how to act in a social situation that didn't have some sort of sexual innuendo behind it. I kept glancing at Tammy, catching her eye once or twice and smiling when she smiled, but other than that I felt paralyzed.

It wasn't until she leaned into me that I started to relax. She asked, "What are you thinking about?" and I sort of hummed and hawed, playing her little game but not giving away any information. I felt that everything that had been happening over the past couple of months was building up to this moment. Right there in my kitchen.

"Come on," she urged. "You can tell me anything."

"I don't think I can tell you this," I answered, and then took a pull off my bottle of beer.

She cocked an eyebrow at me and pursed her lips. "A secret," she whispered. "My, my, this is interesting."

"Yup," I said, nodding and smiling at her. "And it's pretty inappropriate."

"Come on, please. You can tell me anything, I promise. I won't say a word of it to anyone. Just tell me what you're thinking about."

She leaned forward a little further, exposing more of her breasts to me. She tilted her head and offered me her ear to whisper in, and it was in that split second that I just decided to go for it.

I leaned over, placing my mouth just centimeters away from her ear, and put my hand on her bare knee. She sucked in a sharp breath of air at my touch, and I looked down and watched as her chest heaved. Then I whispered...

"I'm thinking that I want to coat my lips in your juices while I lick a thousand times between your legs."

I inched my fingers further up her thigh.

"I'm thinking that I want to feel your mouth wrapped around my cock."

She closed her eyes and moaned the higher up my hand went.

"I'm thinking that I want to feel every inch of myself slide into your tight, wet, pussy, and then I want to pound you so hard you scream louder than you've ever screamed before."

She spread her legs and I cupped my palm

around her mound and rubbed it hard. She grinded against my hand, applying even more pressure, and brought her lips around to meet mine. "Then stop thinking about it and just do it," she whispered. We kissed, and our tongues found one another and coiled around and around as I continued to rub between her legs. I licked down her chin and to her neck, taking her ear lobe in my mouth and sucking on it. She gasped and took my hand from between her legs and placed it on her breast. I immediately tugged one side of her tank top down and under it. She wasn't wearing a bra.

I licked down to her nipple and popped it in my mouth, suckling gently on it as she ran her fingers through my hair. Her skin tasted incredible. I don't know if it was her body wash or perfume or sweat, but whatever it was, it was delicious, and I kept sucking and licking her breast while massaging between Tabby's legs, which she gladly let me do.

"I want to taste all of you," I finally told her. Then I got down on the floor as she pushed her chair away from the table. She spread her legs and I tugged her shorts off and flung them across the room. She laughed and peeled off her tank top, so I took the opportunity to cup both her tits together and lick back and forth between them, all the while feeling the bulge in my pants growing larger and larger.

Without saying another word I got down low and spread her legs apart. She conveniently placed one of them over my shoulder and I slid my tongue up and down her sopping wet slit a few times before resting it on her clit and swirling it around and around. She moaned how good it felt and I looked up to meet her eyes, saying, "You taste so fucking good," and I meant it. She really did have the best pussy I had ever tasted.

She grabbed my hands and put them on her tits, so I licked and tweaked her nipples at the same time, listening to her cries of pleasure when I slid my tongue inside her hole and swirled it around, all the while my nose tickling her clit.

"That feels so fucking good," she said. "Don't stop. I wanna cum."

I did as she asked, removing my hands from her tits and spreading her apart with my thumbs to expose her glistening pink. I paid careful attention to her button while sliding a finger up and inside, curling it around a little to try and hit her G-spot. It must have worked because less than a minute later as I was licking furiously at her pussy, she trembled and shook and gripped a handful of my hair, squeezing it tight, while holding back a scream that came out more as a squeal.

"Oh my fucking fuck," she laughed when it was over. "Holy shit, that was amazing. I don't think I've ever cum that fast before."

I got to my knees and she sat up and took my cheeks in her hands, kissing me hard. "Mmm, you're right," Tabby said, "I do taste good."

I laughed and she stood up, saying, "Now it's my turn."

I stood beside her, drawing her close to me and cupping her ass in my hands while we kissed. It was so soft and pliable, and I ached to pound it.

She fumbled with my belt and the button on my shorts, but eventually got both of them loose and unzipped me. She slid them down and off my feet, and sat me down on the chair she had been on just moments earlier. My cock stood rock hard and ready for her, and Tabby got to her knees and wrapped her tits around it, gliding it up and down between them while making eye contact with me.

"You know what I'm thinking?" she asked with a sly smile.

I shook my head, enjoying the feel of her tits wrapped around my girth.

"I'm thinking I really wanna suck this cock."

"I think that's a great idea," I said.

She kissed me once more on the lips and took me in her small hand, gliding her palm up and down the shaft of my dick while depositing a generous amount of saliva over the head. It dribbled down the side and through her fingers, making a real mess of things. It was fucking awesome.

Tabby sucked me back right down to the root and held her mouth there. I could feel her nose pressing into my groin and let out a groan of satisfaction. I've always loved when girls deepthroat, but not enough of them know how to take a cock all the way down their throats. She came up for air and smiled at me as spit dribbled down her chin.

"You like that?" she teased.

I nodded and guided her mouth back over me. She didn't go down as far, but she did a tremendous job sucking me off. Her lips slid up an down my shaft with ease and I watched every second of it. She looked into my eyes with a mouthful of dick and smiled, reaching underneath it to play with my sac.

"Can't forget about the balls," she purred.

Her tongue traveled down to my scrotum and licked all around the loose skin. She took one nut in her mouth, and then moved on to the other, sucking back each one with gentle care that drove me absolutely nuts, before sliding her tongue back up the underside of my shaft and to the tip of my throbbing knob, which she eagerly gulped back and began sucking once more.

"Jesus Christ," I marveled. "You really know how to suck a dick."

She nodded and mewed but said nothing more. She just kept on gobbling away at my hard rod until I couldn't take it anymore and told her to stop. I didn't want to cum. Not yet anyway. First I had to feel what it was like inside her delicious pussy.

The first chance I got I lifted Tabby to her feet and propped her up on the kitchen table. It's a giant, solid oak piece that I knew would withstand the brunt of a hard fucking, so I wasn't worried about ruining it.

"You naughty boy," she simply said, drawing me in close to her body until her tits were mashed up against my chest. We kissed some more, our mouths open wide and our tongues exploring one another, as I ran my hands all over her smooth, silky skin, which was nice and slick with a coating of sweat that filled the air around us, despite the air conditioning being on nearly full blast.

I laid her back on the table and Tabby spread her legs for me, revealing her ready and waiting pussy that I couldn't wait to fuck.

I slapped the head of my cock off against her slit a few times and tickled her clit with it, causing her to arch her back and cry out with delight. Then, inch by inch, I slid inside her, just like I'd always wanted to.

It was even better than I imagined.

She was way tighter than I expected, and I had to go slowly so it wasn't too painful for her. Tabby took it like a champ though, and when I was all the way in we both gasped with wonder at how good it felt. I leaned over and kissed her neck while slowly pumping away, making sure that my shaft got as slick as it possibly could with her juices before I really started hammering away at that tight snatch. When we both felt we were ready, I stood upright and grabbed hold of her hips.

"Fuck me hard," she commanded.

Not one to disappoint, I began pumping away, drawing Tabby into me with each thrust. Before long, we were furiously going at it, and her tits jiggled and bounced all over the place as I watched my shaft become coated in her juices while my balls slapped against her tight little ass.

She liked the dirty talk, too. "Give it to me," "Fuck me harder," and "I love your fucking cock," were just some of the phrases she cried out repeatedly the more we went at it. Tabby was a little firecracker and it turned me on so much to hear her filthy mouth scream for more because I was happy to give it to her.

I kissed her ankles when she put them against my shoulders, and that made her giggle. She offered me her toes so I sucked on them for a little bit while I kept pumping away at her pussy. She felt so fucking good wrapped around me all nice and snug. It was incredible. The feel of skin on skin and the realization that I was finally fucking my dream girl drove me insane. She had nice feet, too, so I was more than willing to lick and suck her toes for her if that's what turned her on. I enjoyed it just as much as she did.

Leaning over, I cupped her breasts and squeezed them together like before so I could lick her nipples. They were hard and sweaty and she pushed my mouth into her and ran her fingers through my hair while my cock thrust away over and over inside her tight hole. She pulled my head up and stared me in the eyes for a while, smiling and moaning with each solid pounding of my dick.

Looking her in the eyes like that—underneath me all sweaty and naked—was amazing. It was like we both knew what the other person always wanted and now that we were together, it was a fantasy come to life.

"I want to feel you fuck me from behind," she said, not taking her eyes off of mine.

My cock twitched at the thought of ravishing that ass of hers and I pulled out of her pussy, eager to get back in it ASAP. Tabby got on on all fours on the table, so I climbed up behind her and marveled at the shape of her beautiful behind while running my slick hands all over it. I grabbed my cock and guided it back inside her and she cried out with glee at how much deeper it went in that position.

From my vantage point it looked fucking hot. I loved watching her clamped around my shaft as I slid in and out, and the way her asshole winked back at me. I even let my thumb slide over it a few times and she didn't protest, but rather giggled some more at the sensation it gave her.

I knew it couldn't last forever though when I began to feel my balls tighten and the pressure mounting between my legs. I grabbed hold of Tabby's hips and squeezed her tight as I pounded as hard as I fucking could over and over until she came, which left her in a sweaty heap of pleasure beneath me.

"I'm gonna fucking cum soon, baby," I told her.

She moaned and told me to cum on her tits, so I pulled out and hopped down on the floor while she turned over and laid back on the table, arching her back a little and squeezing her breasts together.

I jerked my cock furiously up and down, grunting and groaning, watching as Tabby licked her lips.

"Mmm I can't wait to have your cum all over me," she teased.

That was enough to send me over the edge and I erupted like a volcano all over her skin, shooting hot load after hot load onto her tits. She rubbed my cream in like lotion, spreading it around her skin and over her nipples before licking some of it off her fingers.

"Tastes good," she smiled, grabbing hold of my cock.

She brought it to her mouth and wrapped her lips tight around my twitching head, sucking it back as hard as she could to make sure she got all of my spunk out.

When she was finished she sat up on the table and held me tight as we both calmed down and regained our senses.

"That was amazing," Tabby said. "Maybe next time we can do it in the bed so it's more comfortable."

I kissed her lips and asked, "Is there going to be a next time?"

She nodded and said, "With a cock like that, you bet there is."

It's been almost a month since that day and I still see Tabby and Dale on a regular basis, and while her and I haven't been alone enough to have a second encounter, I know it's coming, and when it does...so will I.

RAMBLINGS

Each issue we feature real letters from real people telling us all about their sexual escapades. Got something spicy to tell us, email it to ramdigest@gmail.com and maybe we'll feature you in an upcoming issue!

SERVICE WITH A SMILE

Hi RAM, thanks for allowing me to write to you. Having someone honest and open to share my experiences with is great. I'm thirty-five and feel kind of juvenile sharing my sexcapades with my buddies, you know? And seeing as how my girlfriend and I love sex, there's a lot to tell. I'll keep this one short, though, and then your readers can let me know if they'd like to hear more. Sound good?

The other night we were out for dinner at a fancy seafood restaurant. Like any fancy place, the lighting was dim and the service sucked, but we had a table tucked away in a corner of the joint, so it felt like we had the entire place to ourselves even though there were people all around us enjoying their food. I ordered some lobster dish and my girlfriend got shrimp. It took forever for the food to come and when it did, it was only subpar. I said for the amount of money we're paying for the dinner, it could at least be hot. My girlfriend just laughed and asked me how hot I wanted it.

Well of course I knew that she was no longer talking about the food, but I didn't know what she had in mind so I just played along, figuring that we'd go back home and fuck each others' brains out after some dirty talk there in the restaurant.

Boy was I wrong.

She scurried over in the booth and sat beside me. As I picked at my plate she ran her hand up my thigh underneath the tablecloth and started rubbing my cock through my slacks. I instantly became hard and put on my poker face so no one would know what was happening. A couple of waiters walked by but didn't suspect a thing because like I said, the lighting was dim and we sort of tucked away, so no one paid us any mind.

As I ate my lobster despite my distain for it, my girlfriend undid my zipper and reached in to pull out my dick right there in the restaurant. Holy shit! We'd fooled it in public places before but never like this. Never where there were a lot of people around.

She started stroking it up and down underneath the table and I took a drink of my water. She made some off the cuff remark, asking if it was hot enough for me now, and I nodded. "Getting there," I said.

Her thumb swirled around my throbbing head as she tugged on me. Her hand felt amazing. When she let go I was disappointed, but the feeling only lasted a moment, as my girlfriend was just adding to the excitement.

She took one of those litte packets of butter and discreetly smeared it in the palm of her hand. When it was lathered up enough, she returned to the scene of the crime, rubbing it all over my dick. Up and down she stroked as the butter basted me like a turkey. Her hand felt so good sliding all over me. She even massaged my balls, which I love! Leaning over, she started whispering things in my ear while she jacked me off. Things like, how I should imagine that it's her mouth all over me, and how she couldn't wait to feel me inside her later. Relay naughty stuff that turned me on so much. I did wish it were her mouth gliding up and down my shaft, and it was true; I wanted to fuck the shit out of her right then and there. I would just have to settle for a hand job now, though, but that was okay.

She nibbled at my earlobe and when our waiter came by to ask how we were doing, she smiled and said fine while I nodded with a mouthful of food, pretending that everything was as normal as could be. He sort of looked at us funny, but he didn't say anything. He left and my girlfriend returned to focusing on my rod.

She told me that she wanted me to cum hard for her. I didn't know what she would do with my hot jizz once it was out of me, but I trusted her judgment. She knew what she was doing and the last thing either of us wanted was to be caught.

I held back for as long as I could, getting a nice build up of sperm in my balls. My dick was so hard and I looked down and lifted the tablecloth to see it covered in butter. My God what a sight! She started jerking it faster and faster and I closed my eyes, imagining all kinds of nasty thing: fucking her in the ass, cumming in her mouth, shoving a dildo up her pussy.

"Come on, baby," she whispered. "Cum for me. Spray that load all over."

I grunted as she squeezed me like I was a tube of toothpaste, and felt the first wave of cum spurt out from my cock. I had no idea where it went or where it landed, just that it felt good to finally have some release. A second rope of thick, juicy jizz exploded out of me, followed by a third and a forth. My cock jerked and spasmed in her hand but she didn't let go. It was incredible.

When my orgasm had subsided, she pulled her hand out from under the table and I saw that it was covered in white, creamy, cum. She laughed and held it above her plate so it could drip down onto what was left of her shrimp. It splashed on the crustaceans and she swirled it all around with her fork. She removed the remainder of the liquid from her hand with a few napkins while I cleaned off my softening dick with a few of my own. I slipped it back in my pants and zipped up, smiling a stupid teenage boy grin. I had just gotten jacked off in a restaurant by a hot chick. It's every guy's fantasy.

Afterward, finished her meal, gobbling down all the shrimp and cum she could eat. At first it was a little gross to watch, but seeing how much she enjoyed it made a difference, not to mention the little slurping sounds she made when she ate.

When we were done, the waiter came and took out plates. Mine still had a bit of lobster on it, but hers was licked clean, literally. She had licked the plate once she was done with her food.

We left and went home to fuck, which we did for the remainder of the night.

So that's my little story for you, RAM. I swear it's all true. You believe me, right? I couldn't make this stuff up if I tried. Anyway, let me know if you want more. In the meantime, my girlfriend and I will be off making more adventures.

Name and location withheld by request

SHARING IS CARING

The first time I ever ate another woman's pussy, I was so nervous.

I knew I was attracted to the ladies, but there's a difference between being 'attracted' and 'having sex' with them. My husband says that he's not afraid to admit when another man is good looking, but that doesn't mean he wants to suck their cock!

Still, it was something I wanted to try, even though I thought it would mean I had to become a full-on lesbian. It never occurred to me that I might be bisexual. I just always thought it was one or the other. Silly me.

Anyway, it was a few years ago, when I was in my early thirties. We had this couple move in next door to us and they were swingers. The whole idea seemed absurd to me, but I couldn't help but find myself drawn to Angela. She was tall and slender, with golden hair and skin as smooth as silk. Over time, I found myself wondering what her pussy tasted like. The first time the thought popped into my head I was freaked out, but I worked up the courage to tell my husband about it and he got really turned on by the idea. Was it possible that we were swingers, too? I doubted it. Passing it off as mere curiosity.

Then one night we had Angela and her husband over for dinner, and they said that they were interested in us. Despite all my desires, it was still a surprise, to both of us. Angela's husband, Don, said I was gorgeous, and she commented on Tony (my husband), saying that he was handsome. They told us more about their lifestyle, and eventually came out saying that they wanted to have sex with us.

Tony and I have always had a generous sex life, doing it four or five times a week while incorporating things like movies and toys, but even this seemed a little too extreme for us. Still, we entertained the thought over desert, and after a few drinks, I mentioned how I was wondering what Angela's cunt was like. Now it was her turn to be surprised. I guess she just automatically assumed I wanted her husband, just like she wanted mine. I elaborated more, going into detail about wanting to taste another woman just once in my life, and to my relief, Angela said she understood, and that she wanted to be my first.

She had one condition, though. The men had to watch.

Well by that time I was feeling pretty good and had no problems with that. So from the dining room we moved to the couch, where her and I began to kiss while Tony and Don sat on the floor in front of us.

Her lips were soft and gentle, and when Angela touched my breast, squeezing it softly, I moaned while our tongues found one another. There was definitely a spark between us, that's for sure. I returned the gesture, squeezing her tits while we still locked lips. When we separated, she peeled off her top and took of her bra, and I immediately went down to suckle one of her nipples. It got rock hard in my mouth as my hand traveled down to her crotch to massage her mound, which was already steaming with anticipation.

She unbuttoned her slacks and I helped her get them off, revealing a pair of lacey white panties that had a damp spot in the middle. Oh my! I got down on the floor as she spread her legs wide, and I deposited tiny kisses up and down the inside of her thighs until my lips came to rest on her underwear-covered pussy. I was shaking all over and Tony came up behind me and placed his hands on my shoulders. "It's okay," he said. "Let me help."

He took one side of Angela's panties while I took the other, and together we removed them from her, and I got a glimpse of her snatch for the first time. It was smooth and shaved and when she spread her legs again her lips parted a bit and I saw just how wet she really was. I got in close to take a whiff and she smelled amazing. Tony rested on the couch beside her and she relaxed a leg on his lap. He help her open for me as I took the plunge and touched my lips to hers, then slowly licked her slit.

I won't say I enjoyed the taste right of the bat, but the more I played with her sweet pussy, the more I got used to it. I parted her labia with my thumbs and continued to lick all around her, paying close attention to her clit. From there I slid my tongue inside her hole and she squirmed while running a hand through my hair. It was intense, and I soon found myself lost in the moment, fucking her with my tongue while her clit bounced off my nose. My chin was covered in her wetness as I furiously moved my face around, wanting to make sure I covered all her parts. I glanced over at Tony, and he smiled down at me.

I continued to poke and suck her pussy, closing my eyes and enjoying the hell out of it. Her juices flowed down my throat and I reached up to caress her tits while I ate her out. She took my hands in hers and cried out when I tweaked her nipples.

After a few more moments she screamed that she was going to cum, and I found myself extremely pleased with my efforts. My first time out and I made a girl cum! I quickly did one last thing that I had been wanting to do, and that's slide a finger inside her while I nibbled with my lips on her clit. I worked it in and out of her, fingering her with glee as I munched on her nub. She trembled and shook and threw her head back in ecstasy, and when she came, I replaced my finger with my mouth and tongue, wanting to get the full flavor of her juices. Angela trembled and pushed my face deep into her cunt so that I could barely breathe, but I continued to suck at her hole, taking all of her down my throat. She tasted so good, just like I had been hoping.

When she was done, she collapsed and smiled down at me, brushing a hair out of my face. "That was wonderful," she said. I wiped my chin and agreed with her. The four of us laughed, and Tony and Don clapped, applauding my efforts.

Since then we've spent a great deal of time with Angela and Don, and eventually I let him fuck the shit out of me, while Tony had his way with Angela. I wouldn't call us full-blown swingers now, more like experimenters. They're the only couple we've been with, and for now we're good with that.

I hope you liked my confession, RAM. I think I was just as nervous writing it down for you as I was the day it happened. Now that I got it out, though, I feel much better, and hopefully your readers do too!

Best,
Amanda
Glens Falls, NY

CHANGING IT UP

My wife and I have only been married for a year but I just wanted to share a quick encounter that we had last week.

We were out shopping for clothes and my wife was trying on dresses in a department store. Like a good husband I was nodding and agreeing with everything she said, and complimenting her on how she looked. Well she must have noticed me placating her because before too long she was acting all naughty, trying harder to get my wandering attention. It worked! She began sliding the dresses up her leg, secretly showing me more of her thigh before ducking back into the change room to try on another one, where she would do the same thing, only as time progressed and she tried on more and more dresses, she'd lift them higher and higher, always making sure that no one was watching.

Not to brag or anything, but my wife is a looker, too, so seeing her act that way in a public place just got me so horny. What could I do though? We were in a freakin' department store! I thought she was just prepping me for later and that when we got home she'd surely jump my bones, but as it turned out she had other ideas.

After a couple of more mini fashion/strip shows, she winked and nodded for me to follow her into the change rooms. It was a slow day and there weren't many people around, but still, was she really asking what I thought she was? I looked left and right and over my shoulder, and when the coast was clear I followed her back and got in the little box with her, locking the door behind me.

"I want you to fuck the shit out of me," she whispered in my ear, darting her tongue out to lick my lobe.

"Here?" I asked.

"Uh huh," she bit her bottom lip in that way she does that drives me nuts, and rapidly blinked her eyes.

I didn't have to be asked twice.

I kissed her, hard, and slid my hands up the dress she had on, squeezing her ass tight. My thumbs found her panties and yanked them down as she fumbled with my belt buckle. I was so fucking hard, I thought I was going to cum before she even got my pants down around my ankles. I held back though, wanting nothing more than to feel her vice-like pussy wrapped around my man meat.

With my dick swaying back and forth in the air, she licked the palm of her hand and jerked me off for a bit, teasing the head of my throbbing cock with her fingers, all the while staring directly into me eyes. From there she turned around and lifted the dress around her hips, exposing her beautiful, smooth bottom to me. I guided my cock into her sopping wet mound, and she splashed her hands against the change room wall, grunting as I entered her.

I slowly pumped in and out of her pussy, trying to be as quiet as a mouse so we wouldn't alert any of the department store staff. The last thing I needed was for someone to bust in and see me fucking my wife. I love sex, but I'm not ready to go to jail over it.

I looked down to see my dick covered in her juices, and that got me even harder. My pulsating head bounced against her cervix and I reached around to fondle her wonderful tits while she grinded her ass back against me, taking me in as deep as she could. From her tits I moved my hands down to between her legs, and gently rubbed her clit as my cock continued to pound her. She mewed a little and I whispered, "Shhh," in her ear. She nodded and clenched her lips together to prevent herself from making any further noise.

Being there with her like that, in a department store change room, just got me so riled up. Normally I like to take my time and enjoy sex, but something like that you have to do quickly or else risk being caught. Seeing her ass move in waves as I slapped against her was perfect, though, and it wasn't too much longer before I felt that I was going to explode. I told her as such, whispering, "I'm going to cum." She looked back over her shoulder and smiled at me. "Cum inside me," she said. "Cum in my pussy."

Usually cum is something she likes to enjoy seeing, but this time was different. If I pulled out and jizzed all over her ass or face, we had no way to clean it up, so I could see why she would have wanted to keep it concealed deep inside her folds. I nodded, knowing that she takes birth control, and after a few more pumps my dick spasmed inside of her as it let loose a surge of cum so big I thought she would overflow with cream.

We both panted as my dick began to soften inside of her. I pulled out and yanked my boxers and jeans back on while she got dressed in her street clothes. Not a word was said between us, but there didn't' need to be. I knew she had enjoyed it, and by the look on my face, she knew that I did too.

When we were both dressed, she peeked her head out of the change room to make sure no one was looking. When she gave me the all clear we quickly exited the changing area only as we came around a corner, there was a department store worker standing there looking at us both. His head went back and forth between us like he was watching a tennis match, but before he could say a word we both laughed and scampered off like thieves in the night.

RAM, it was such an amazing experience and when we got home we tore each other's clothes off and went at it again, still horny from the encounter in the change room.

So thank you again for letting me write to you. I just wanted you guys to know that what you do is appreciated. As long as you keep publishing your digest, my wife and I will keep reading.

Best,
Glenn R.
Rochester, NY

TIPS & TRICKS

We here at RAM Digest are all about the sexy sex...obviously. We love to fuck, and we love reading about hot men and women getting fucked. Chances are that if you're reading this, you love getting fucked, too!

But have you ever wanted to improve your skills in the bedroom? Have you ever thought about how you could become a better lover to your mate? Of course you have. It's perfectly normal to want to better yourself in all aspects of life. From your job and friendships, to your relationships and sex—we all strive to be the best we can be.

That's why our panel of sexperts have come up with a nifty little way to help you out in the bedroom.

Each issue we're going to be bringing you a tip or trick to use in the sack that will be sure to please whomever you are bedding. These are tested and true methods used by our staff to drive their partners crazy!

So without further ado, RAM Digest is pleased to offer you its first tip, brought to you by our Managing Copy Editor, Alanna Mansfield (yes, we do have women on staff here):

"Hello from the trenches of RAM Digest. I'm Alanna Mansfield, and I've been asked to provide a sex tip for the very first issue that you are holding in your hands.

You guys like sex, right? I sure do, and one of my most favorite things is foreplay. All that touching, licking, and sucking drives me wild, so that when a guy slides his nice hard cock inside me, I'm already so turned on that I cum in no time.

One of the most important aspects of foreplay though, and something that a lot of people overlook, is the dirty talk. I don't know if it's because they feel embarrassed or are just shy, but a lot of guys I'm with don't say too much when we're in the process of fooling around.

Personally, I love it when a man talks dirty to me in the bedroom, and I'm betting a lot of other women out there love it to. There's just something so hot and naughty about a guy telling me what he's going to do to me, or what he loves about my body.

So for you men out there reading this, here's my tip for you: when you go down on a woman (and you should ALWAYS go down on a woman), tell her how good she tastes, and how much you love her pussy.

It'll drive her nuts.

Seriously. Women like to feel confident about their genitals just as much as you do, so when you tell her how good her pussy looks and tastes, it'll give her the confidence she needs to perhaps open up and try different kinds of sexual activity, like various positions, toys, anal, etc. Not only that, but she's also more likely to orgasm knowing that her nether parts are driving you wild with lust.

So lick, suck, and finger all you want, but don't forget that when you're down there, make sure you tell your girl that you're having a good time. Mention to her how much you love her pussy, tell her how fucking good she tastes...I bet she'll be screaming in no time.

I know I do."

Wow! Thanks for that awesome tip, Alanna. Wise up, men, and listen to what she's saying. She's definitely correct in saying that women like to feel confident about their genitals just as much as you guys do. It turns them on, and makes them feel sexy. So give it a try and let us know how you do.

Feel free to email us with the results at ramdigest@gmail.com. Who knows, we might even feature your responses in an upcoming issue.

Until next time...

"Sex is a part of nature. I go along with nature."
- Marilyn Monroe

Printed in Great Britain
by Amazon

26934020R00059